Other Golden City Books

by J. Kathleen Cheney

AFTER THE WAR

A TALE OF *THE GOLDEN CITY*

J. KATHLEEN CHENEY

EQP Books

AFTER THE WAR

An EQP Book / 2016

UUID# F12CCBA3-DC87-46B5-829C-1A819852B95B

For information address the author at:

http://jkathleencheney.com

Editing and formatting by:

E-QUALITY PRESS

The name E-QUALITY PRESS and the logo consisting of
the letters "EQP" over an open book with power cord are
registered trademarks of E-QUALITY PRESS.

http://EQPbooks.com/

PRODUCED IN THE UNITED STATES OF AMERICA

ACKNOWLEDGEMENTS

THANKS TO everyone who's helped out on this story: to all those who read early copies and gave commentary; to my cover artist, Rachel A. Marks, who always does the most lovely work for me (despite having a dozen other hats to wear); to Rick Fisher, who's valiantly edited my work and helped me with a thousand side issues in publishing; and to my Patreon supporters, who helped bring this story to the page.

CONTENTS

AFTER THE WAR

CHAPTER 1

Friday, 18 June 1920, Lisboa

THE CAFÉ MARTINHO DA ARCADA at the Praça do Commercio had a sign in their window, advertising that Serafim Palmeira would be singing there that evening. As João da Silva had actually heard one of the other street workers speak of her lovely, mournful voice, he'd made up his mind that he would spend a few of his hard earned mil-reís and go hear her. So, after a long day of working on a mosaic on Santa Augusta Street, he returned to his tiny rented room in the Barrio Alto, cleaned up as best he could and dressed in his Sunday finest. Then he made the trek back down to the Baixa, the city's modern downtown.

He was learning to love Lisboa. The night was sultry, with the scent of the sea drifting in from the mouth of the slow-moving Tagus. The sky was clear, although the stars seemed dim next to the bright shine of the City of Light. At night the Baixa glowed with electric streetlamps. Pedestrians in fine garb walked along the street, the cheerful chatter of groups distracting João as he walked past, hands shoved in his pockets, trying not to see others' lax handling of their handbags and wallets.

Portugal felt like home to him, but it was in places like this where he was most alone. He had no one to walk with, no one to talk to. He had no past, and couldn't seem to trust others.

There was still much in life to enjoy. Once he'd reached the café, he joined the press of bodies near the bar to order a Vinho Verde, and then stood against the wall with those waiting to hear the visiting singer. At the moment, a man sat in the corner, playing the twelve-stringed guitar, the tune speaking of loss and pain. It felt familiar to João, the way everything about sorrow resonated with him. He'd often wondered if that was why he loved *fado*—the music of love and loss.

He knew loss, if nothing else.

Another man, not as well bathed, and reeking of onions, bumped João's shoulder, trying to claim another space against the wall. He stood so close that João felt the man's wallet in a jacket pocket. He could lift it out if he chose.

He was looking at the interloper when the singer walked to the chair next to the guitarist. When João turned back, Serafim Palmeira sat there, her slim figure wrapped in an old fashioned costume, a white cotton shirt and black skirt, with a simple black shawl draped about her shoulders. Her hair was short, in the current fashion, with inky black curls. One pale hand lay atop her shawl, the other in her lap, the webbing between her fingers barely visible from where he stood across the hall.

He might like *fado*, but this was why he'd come to see her. She was a *sereia*.

The sereia didn't come to Lisboa—they feared the city was cursed—but supposedly Miss Palmeira was a Christian like João and not given to superstition.

He sipped at his wine, eyes drifting closed as she sang her first notes.

Her voice was soft but carried throughout the long café's hall, such yearning in it that tears stung in João's eyes. She sang of lost love, of losing her man, something she knew despite her youth. She couldn't be more than twenty, but it was said she'd lost her husband in the Great War. The pain in her voice was clear.

That song ended, and she promptly launched into another. João found himself staring at her, unsure when he'd opened his eyes. Her face was lowered, her wide dark eyes fixed on the café's tiled floor. Her shawl had slipped a bit, and her gill slits showed on the side of her neck, further proof that she wasn't human. If she was using her *call* to make her song more poignant, João couldn't tell, but he doubted she needed that magic.

Her eyes lifted then as she sang of the beauty of the Golden City, her home, and for the first time she gazed out over her audience. Tears glistened in her dark eyes as she sang of the anguish of wanting to be home, but *not* wanting to be there alone. Her eyes drifted across the mass of lower mortals by the café's door.

And she stopped singing, one webbed hand pressed to her heart. She looked . . . shocked.

The crowd went silent, all aware something had gone awry.

She stepped down from the dais and darted toward the café's door, as if she had to escape. She cried a name as she pelted across the floor, but when she neared the door, she veered aside, slipping around one of the tables and nearly knocking an old man onto the floor. She didn't even apologize, but strove forward, pushing through the crowd of men in her desperation to reach . . .

Me.

João wasn't sure whether to run or not. Her eyes were fixed on his, confusion in them.

"Alejandro!" she cried again. Enough men cleared aside that she could grab the lapels of João's tatty jacket. "Alejandro. What. . . ?"

And then she swooned.

Unable to do anything less, João caught her in his arms. He gazed down at the young woman's pale face. He didn't recognize her. Not at all. Did she know *him?* Or had she, in her sorrow, convinced herself he was someone she'd known?

The guitarist had pursued the young woman across the hall, an older man with streaks of gray in his black hair. He regarded João with equal disbelief. "Jandro? What are you doing here?"

João stared. "Do you know me, sir?"

The man seemed startled. "Do you not recognize me, Jandro?"

For a split second, João's head swam, and he thought he might swoon as well. *Did* he know these people? He gazed down at the girl in his arms, whose eyes began to flutter. "I have no memory, sir," he told the older man, glancing up. "I was injured in the war and have no memory of *anything* before that."

The man reached across the girl's body to cup João's cheek like he was family. "You are Alexandre Ferreira, my daughter's husband."

His brain supplied the information that Alexandre was a Portuguese form of Alejandro, but neither name meant anything to him. He turned his eyes back down to meet those of Serafim Palmeira, who pulled away to gaze at him, tears running down her pale cheeks. *How could I possibly have forgotten being married to a girl like this?*

"Alejandro," she whispered, laying her webbed hands against his cheeks. "I knew you weren't dead. I knew when they told me that . . . it was a lie."

If she'd been alone, he would have thought her insane, but the man with her—surely her father—seemed to believe her claim. A father wouldn't support her in madness, would he?

João glanced up, suddenly aware of the commotion all about them, people staring and someone with a camera trying to take a photograph in the darkened café. He raised his hand to shield his face just before the brilliant flash. *I need to get out of this place.* He drew away from the young woman's grip, but she grabbed his lapels again. "Miss," he insisted, "if you want to talk to me, it should be *elsewhere.*"

"Alejandro," she began.

"I don't know you," he said firmly. "I don't recognize you."

Her expression went stricken.

"Jandro," the older man said, reaching past his daughter to grasp João's elbow, "come with us backstage. We can talk privately there."

He could toss off the man's grasp, but something in the older man's face pleaded for him to stay, to talk to them. Ignoring his instincts, João went with them, behind the stage where someone from the café's staff was apologizing to the crowd for the interruption. Down a small hallway, a single door led into a sitting area.

The room was shabby compared to the rest of the café. João felt less out of place there. The young woman, Serafim, clung to his arm fiercely as if she never intended to let him go. João found himself gazing at the webbed fingers on his sleeve and realized he'd been staring. "Pardon me," he said quickly, flushing.

She didn't seem to grasp why he'd apologized.

"Please, sit down," her father said.

João complied, and the girl surprised him by settling on the floor next to his knees. She laid her head on his lap, weeping softly again. João set his hand atop her head, the black curls under his fingers not familiar at all. Her hair wasn't short after all, he noted, but pinned up in back. He wondered what it would look like down around her shoulders. His heart beat harder at that thought, but he forced his attention back to her father. "Sir, I don't know either of you."

The man dragged over a wooden chair and sat facing João. Apparently the sight of his daughter draped over a stranger's legs didn't concern him. João kept his surprise to himself. He was the one at a disadvantage here. There *was* a chance these two were exactly who they claimed.

If only his mind would supply an answer . . . yet it remained annoyingly blank.

"My name is Marcos Davila," the man said. "And this is my eldest daughter, Serafim Palmeira. Do you not recognize either of us, Jandro?"

"No," he repeated. "I was wounded in the war. I have no memories." Why did he have to keep repeating that?

"We were told you were killed at La Lys," Davila said, "but the body returned to us could not have been yours. We hoped . . . Joaquim was sure they'd made a mistake."

Serafim rubbed her face against João's thighs, distracting him. It was an innocent gesture, yet appallingly familiar. Then again, she thought she was his wife, didn't she?

"Why do you say it could not have been my body?" he asked Davila.

Davila shook his head wearily. "The body was terribly burned all over, save the bottom of the man's feet. Those feet were human."

João licked his lips. Davila didn't have webbed hands. That didn't necessarily mean he was human. "Are you claiming that I'm *not* human?"

"You're *half* human, Jandro," Davila said, "like me. You have the markings of a sereia, though. That alone should have told the army they were wrong; but, apparently, it wasn't on your records."

João took a deep breath. Suddenly the chance that this man was telling the truth rose. Unlike Serafim, Alejandro had no webbing between his fingers and no gill slits on the side of his neck. He'd decided to keep the inhuman coloration of the lower half of his body hidden, secret since it was one thing that *would* help him identify his family. That wasn't difficult, as he merely needed to keep his clothes and shoes on.

"Please, Alejandro," Serafim begged, "please say you know me."

He gazed down at her, his lips pressed together. He desperately *wanted* to recognize this beautiful girl. "I'm sorry, Miss Serafim. I don't."

She pushed herself away from him and rose to her feet, crossing her arms over her chest. "No. I won't accept that. You *know* me, Alejandro. You came back to me, and I will not let you go again."

Her sudden vehemence startled him. She didn't stamp her foot, but he suspected she was close to that point. "Miss, I . . ."

"Father, will you leave us for a moment?"

Davila opened his mouth, but shrugged and walked out of the sitting room, leaving João at his daughter's mercy.

As soon as the door closed, the girl flung herself into João's arms, her lips pressing hard against his as if she intended to devour him. He didn't know what else to do, so he set his hands on her waist and held her away from him.

"You cannot say you don't know my kiss," she said, chin firming as she met his gaze.

Actually, I can. That had been no more familiar than anything else about her.

She was lovely, though, and he liked the feel of her in his arms. There hadn't been a woman since the war; he hadn't known who he was and feared he had a wife and five children somewhere. He certainly wouldn't *dislike* it if Serafim Palmeira turned out to be that wife.

"Should I prove it?" she asked tartly. "Your dorsal stripe turns dark blue at the edges, not like mine, which is pure black. The edging is darker than mine, too, almost a navy blue, and its point extends right up underneath . . ."

She went on to describe the inhuman coloration of his privates with a level of detail that João suspected could *only* come from firsthand knowledge. For a moment it was hard to breathe, embarrassment warring with surprise for control of his reaction. If this girl was his wife, she was shockingly forward. Did he *like* that about her? Or was it not forwardness if she was truly his wife?

He took a step back, trying to think. Did all sereia have the same markings? Could she just have generalized and guessed correctly?

She pursued him and her hand touched the inside of his thigh. "Do you have a scar here? You were hit by shrapnel in Angola and were still healing the last time we were together."

He did have a scar there, exactly where her fingers touched. And as it was close to the area she'd been describing in detail a moment before, her gesture gained his body's full attention. Her hand moved slightly, and this time when she kissed him, he was no longer in a mood to escape. He pulled her closer. Her arms wrapped tightly around him, the kiss deepening into something *wholly* inappropriate if she wasn't his wife.

A knock on the door warned him a second before the door opened. Her father stepped back into the room. João—he'd known that wasn't his name, but it would surely take time to get used to any other—João turned Serafim loose and prayed to God that his arousal would subside before the girl's father noticed. Fortunately, she stood between him and Davila.

He'd always believed that if he found someone from his past, he would recall everything. That he would *know* in his heart. Yet to know him as well as she did, Serafina must have been his lover at some point. Even so, there was nothing in him that recognized her, and he had a feeling she didn't want to hear him say that again.

"I think we should go back to the hotel, Father," she said. "Alejandro and I need to talk. Can you make my apologies to the manager here?"

Her father's eyes drifted past her to meet his, as if to ask whether the plan met with his approval.

João—Alejandro—nodded. Or was it Alexandre? Why would he have a Portuguese name *and* a Spanish name?

Serafim reached back and wrapped her hand around his—no lacing of fingers because of her webbing. A moment later she was hauling him through the main room of the café straight out onto a street where she hailed a cab. Her father joined them at the edge of the sidewalk, and soon they were at the Hotel Avenida Palace, a place far more opulent than he would have been able to afford himself.

Before her father could protest, Serafim grabbed his hand, dragged him upstairs into a room, and closed the door behind them. João—Alejandro—barely had time to glance around before she turned on him. "Where have you been?" she demanded.

Finally, she was going to listen to *him*. "I was in a hospital in France for a long time." It hadn't actually been a hospital, but a sanitarium for veterans, a place for those men driven past reason by the war. "No one knew who I was. They thought I must be French, but . . ."

"Why would they think you *French?*" she asked, looking offended.

"Because they spoke to me in French, and I answered them so." It hadn't taken him long to decide that although he was moderately fluent in it, French wasn't his mother tongue.

"Why were you in a French hospital?"

"I assume I was in France for the war," he told her. "I've no idea."

"Then why didn't you come home?"

Is she always this difficult? "Because I didn't know where home *was,*" he snapped. "If I'd known where to go, don't you think I would have done so years ago?"

Tears started in her eyes again. She came and put her arms around him. "I'm so sorry, Alejandro."

She raised her face to his, and this time he kissed her before she could kiss him.

I am going to hell.

He'd woken in Serafim's arms, feeling he'd done something illicit.

He slid away from her and out of the bed, stopping to peer down at her sleeping form. He hoped to heaven she was his wife. Evidence certainly upheld her claim, as she knew his body far better than any woman save a wife should. Even so, he felt guilty for bedding a woman he'd just met. Sighing, he headed for the bathroom. The electric lights there were startlingly bright, and he stared at his reflection, wondering who this Alexandre Ferreira actually was.

Are you Alexandre? he asked that face in the mirror. *Are you Alejandro?*

Neither name sounded like his. But *nothing* had so far, not in two years.

He spoke Spanish, English, and French well but simply didn't have the vocabulary in those tongues that he had in Portuguese. That was why he'd slowly made his way to Portugal. Lisbon had been his first stop in the country, and he'd found work quickly enough. Menial labor, but it paid for meals and a tiny room. He'd been comfortable. The need to flee he'd felt in other locations hadn't crept over him yet.

Perhaps this *was* home, this or the Golden City.

He stared at his face in the mirror. He wanted this life. He wanted *her* to be his wife. It was seductive not to question his good fortune, or the sheer coincidence of running into her in a café on a night when she happened to be singing there.

"Alejandro?" Serafim's soft voice called.

He quickly washed his hands and returned to the bedroom. Serafim held up the sheets for him to rejoin her, and he went, willingly. She came into his arms, her warm body pressing against his chilled skin. Her long hair tangled about him as if it had a life of its own. She kissed him, and whispered, "Say my name, Alejandro."

"Serafim," he said softly, willing to please her.

She shook her head, pulling away. "No, my *real* name."

"Serafina," he answered.

Her arms came about him again. "I knew you remembered."

No, he hadn't remembered. It had been logic, a good guess, no more. She called him by the Spanish version of his name, so he simply chose the Spanish version of hers. Why should they not both have Spanish names? But she had long since moved past talking, her hands on him again, her lips on his throat, chasing all else from his mind.

Saturday, 19 June 1920, Lisboa

He was going to be Alejandro Ferreira until he had a better understanding of the situation.

He didn't want to hurt Serafina. She would make a charming, if sometimes vexing, wife. Demanding, likely exhausting, but from all appearances utterly devoted to him.

So Alejandro bathed and dressed in his worn garb, ruefully reflecting that he would be the worst dressed man in the hotel's restaurant that morning. He walked down the stairs with a smiling Serafina on his arm, and was greeted like a long-lost son by Marcos Davila, even though the man couldn't know whether he'd spent the night talking with his daughter . . . or bedding her.

The restaurant was a place of white-draped tables. Wealthy people already sat at some, easily discernable by their lack of concern about their possessions. *Foolish.* A few businessmen were there, one table apparently railroad men. One man was a former soldier. An officer, Alejandro guessed, judging by his demeanor and the narrow scar over one temple. His stiff carriage hinted at a back injury as well. No threats, Alejandro decided as he followed his newfound family into the dining room.

"Will you please tell me, sir," Alejandro began after they'd settled at a white-draped table. "How comes it that my name is Spanish?"

"You were born in Spain," Davila said, "as was Serafina. I am Spanish, as well."

Alejandro licked his lips. The Spanish didn't have much use for sereia, the result of a horrible scandal nearly two decades ago. They had long memories. How would a sereia like Serafina and a half-sereia like himself fare in Spain? "Are you. . . ?"

His question was cut short when Davila's eyes lifted. The man gazed past Alejandro and a wide smile of relief lightened his features. Alejandro turned to look over his shoulder. An older man walking with an ebony cane approached their table, his eyes both cautious and hopeful. Without thinking, Alejandro rose to his feet, breath held tight.

The older man—perhaps fifty or so—had *his* face.

It was the same face Alejandro saw in the mirror: square jaw, wide forehead, straight brown hair, and darker skin than many Portuguese. Straight nose, although it had clearly been broken at least once. The man had some gray hair at his brow and a limp that spoke of an old injury. His suit was well made without being flashy. Something about him said *police officer* to Alejandro. The man removed his hat as he approached the table and stepped forward to embrace Alejandro, then kissed his cheeks.

"Sir?" Alejandro said. "I . . ." He didn't know what to say. As the older man stepped back, he finally managed, "Are you my father?"

The man glanced aside, and Alejandro noted for the first time that he hadn't come alone. A second man was with him, a mestiço with skin of medium brown and smoky green eyes, both men near the same age.

"This *is* Alejandro," the mestiço man pronounced.

"I had no doubt," the first man replied, and turned back to Alejandro. "I'm your brother, Joaquim Tavares. Marcos told me you've lost your memory."

Ah, there must have been a telephone call placed to the Golden City, summoning this man.

"Why don't we sit down and eat?" the mestiço man suggested.

Waiters came and rearranged their chairs for them, then whisked off to retrieve water and coffee for the newcomers. Alejandro used that time to marshal his thoughts, and Serafina reached under the tablecloth to grasp his hand.

That man is *my brother*. Joaquim Tavares looked too much like him to be anything else, despite the differing surnames and the gap in age. Joaquim even had similar hand motions, and cocked his head in the same way.

"That was done magically," the mestiço man pronounced as soon as the waiters were gone. "The memory cap, I mean. A hex—a combination of curse and witchcraft. Not an injury. That has to be why you couldn't find him, Joaquim. The memory loss effectively changes who he is, even to the perception of your gift. It's also suppressing his gift. I can't see it right now, but I'm sure it's still there."

Alejandro kept his mouth shut, his general response when uncertain. Safer to say nothing. The fact that his missing memory was the result of a hex rather than an injury had to be a hopeful sign, though.

Serafina squeezed Alejandro's hand. "Can you fix it, Uncle?"

She'd asked that of the mestiço man. He turned a sardonic expression on her. "And how would I be able to do that, girl?"

"Surely you know someone who can fix it," she insisted. "One of those Freemasons, right?"

They were discussing witchcraft like it was a normal table topic. Alejandro pressed his lips together.

"I can ask around," the man said, "but you know very well that witchcraft is illegal."

Serafina pouted dramatically, and the man seemed to accept *that* as normal as well.

"Can we all pause for a moment?" Joaquim asked. "Alejandro, this is Inspector Gaspar of the Special Police. He's known you since you were a child, and taught you to play football."

Alejandro peered at Gaspar for a moment, wondering if anything about him would stir a memory, but it didn't. He turned back to Joaquim. "Sir, I don't understand. What gift is he talking about?"

"You're a seer, Alejandro," Joaquim said. "A rather profound one, I should add, but it appears that didn't stop you from being hexed at some point."

"Well, we have to fix it," Serafina insisted again.

"I, for one, am simply happy he's still alive," Joaquim told her with fatherly sternness. "Marina will be overjoyed just to have him home."

Serafina pouted again, clearly unhappy with being told to be satisfied with what she had. Her father didn't protest Joaquim's commentary on his daughter, which suggested that Davila agreed. Alejandro let his eyes drift to the table.

Joaquim doesn't think they can fix me. It was a chilling realization.

He hadn't expected anyone to fix him . . . not until Serafina said something. Her simple request had raised hopes he'd thought long since dead. Alejandro took a breath and licked his lips.

"Um, Marina?" he asked, hoping he didn't have a girlfriend as well as a wife.

"My wife," Joaquim said, "who raised you after your mother departed."

Departed. That made it sound like his mother had left this earth via train. "I see."

Joaquim chuckled. "I suspect we're overwhelming you with new information, Alejandro. It might be easier if you and I spoke alone. I can tell you whatever you want about your past, save for the last few years, of course."

That was reassuring. Someone was *finally* going to tell him who Alejandro Ferreira was. He hoped that would tell him how to act around these people and what they expected of him. "Thank you, sir."

Alejandro spent a few hours closeted with Joaquim, learning his own history and that of his rather convoluted family. He had two living older brothers, and each of them had different mothers. Only Duilio, the eldest, was legitimate, and *his* mother was a selkie. Joaquim was the product of a liaison with a young woman in Barcelona, just as Alejandro himself was, although his own mother had been a *sereia* woman. That left Alejandro with a rather low opinion of the fidelity of the man who'd sired the three of them.

It was clear, though, that Joaquim had stepped in to raise him. If nothing else, Alejandro wished his memory back so that he could better know this man—and his wife Marina, who'd become Alejandro's second mother.

Joaquim went on to tell him that his birth mother had been a prisoner in Spain, as had Serafina's. The two sereia women were among a couple dozen sold into virtual slavery by their own government. They'd been rescued and given their freedom when Alejandro was only seven, and Serafina just a toddler.

Apparently, he'd known Serafina since her birth. "And now she is my wife."

Joaquim shifted in his chair, setting his cane aside. "More or less."

Alejandro's stomach sank. "What does that mean?"

"Just that . . . things slipped during the Great War," Joaquim answered. "You came back from Angola, but had only three days before you shipped out to France. Marina and I barely saw you in that time. Afterward, Serafina said that the two of you had married, but we never saw any evidence of that. There's no license or records of a church marriage."

God help me. Alejandro covered his face with his hand. "Am I the sort of man who would treat a woman that way?"

Joaquim held his hands wide. "No. And the fact that you just asked should prove that to you. I should have been clearer, though. Because you both also have sereia citizenship, *legally* all that's needed there is a verbal agreement between you."

"So our marriage is legal on the sereia islands," he guessed, "but not here?"

"I think that's the best interpretation. You're married, but not in the eyes of the State or the Church. When Marina asked Serafina about it, she became very defensive. It's a delicate topic, and we didn't want to press her."

Alejandro puffed out his cheeks. "She doesn't have a wedding ring."

"She can't wear one," Joaquim pointed out, "so you wouldn't have purchased one for her anyway."

Ah, yes, the webbing. She hadn't worn any rings because she *couldn't.* "She wouldn't have received any benefits from the army if something happened to me, would she?"

"No," Joaquim said, "but you knew we would never let anything happen to her. Her family and ours have always been close."

His mother and Serafina's had been prisoners together, and her father and Joaquim had shared a prison cell at one point. That must have forged a bond. Still, Alejandro hated the idea that he'd taken a wife—legally or not—and hadn't provided for her. "We don't have any children, do we?"

"No." A smile crept across Joaquim's serious features. "Isn't that something you should have asked *her*?"

Alejandro dragged a hand across his forehead. "Every time we start to talk, we end up . . . *not* talking."

Joaquim chuckled. "I suppose I can understand, since she's not seen you in so long. Remember, Serafina isn't missing any memories, so this is a completely different situation for her than it is for you. I suspect you'll need to be patient."

"Because she won't be?" He'd been in her company for less than a day, and he knew that much.

"No, Serafina's never been a patient girl," Joaquim told him.

"But I did *intend* to marry her," Alejandro asked cautiously. "Didn't I?"

"Yes. You'd known for years that you would. That's one reason there wasn't more of a fuss when her parents realized there was no proof of your wedding. They trusted that you would make good on any promise. You've always been the responsible one."

Good to know I'm viewed as responsible, at least. He would hate to find a family only to learn they despised him for some moral weakness. He certainly didn't intend to back out of any relationship he had with Serafina. "I should start working on a church wedding, then."

"Her parents would appreciate that," Joaquim said with another smile. "It's like you to try to take care of Serafina first and only then worry about yourself. We do need to find out what happened to you."

Alejandro regarded him frankly. "You don't think this can be fixed, though, do you?"

Joaquim rubbed a hand over his face, looking suddenly tired. "I've worked with the Special Police for a very long time, Alejandro. My experience says that anything done by witchcraft can only be undone by witchcraft. That's an option not open to us."

Because the Church forbade witchcraft, as did the State. It was different from *witchery*, the use of talents that occurred naturally, like being a seer or a finder or whatever it was that Gaspar did. They were *witches*, but so long as they didn't attempt to augment their talents illicitly, the Church allowed them to live in peace. *Witchcraft*, on the other hand, required spells and usually sacrifice of some kind; *that* was what the Church forbade. The fine line between the two could be debated, but apparently his particular problem was clearly on the wrong side of that line.

"So I'm stuck with this. With starting all over again."

"Yes," Joaquim said. "Unless we find something that tells us differently. Unfortunately, since Gaspar says it's a hex, the only witch who can remove it is the same witch who laid it on you. I will be here, though, any time you need to talk. Anything I can do, I will."

Alejandro gazed at him for a moment. Unlike anyone he'd met in the last two and a half years, Alejandro *trusted* the man. Not because he recognized him. He still had no spark of memory regarding Joaquim. But Joaquim looked so much like what Alejandro saw in the mirror that there was no room for doubt. "I do appreciate that, brother. Do. . . ?"

Joaquim's head tilted. "What else?"

"Do I have any profession? I've been a laborer since the hospital, but . . . all I seem to recognize is . . . how to steal." He felt himself flush even mentioning that.

Joaquim patted his shoulder. "You were raised in a prison, Alejandro, and learned young to pick pockets. To my knowledge, you haven't done so since, save as a parlor trick. It's always been a point of pride for you that you no longer steal. As for profession, you'd begun your studies at Coimbra. You had some intention of becoming a writer, but then the war broke out."

"A poet?" he asked, hoping the answer was *no*. "Or a newspaper writer?"

Joaquim chuckled at his obvious discomfort. "No, you always wrote stories of adventure. Like the works of Haggard and Wells and Verne. As soon as you learned to write, you and your cousin Miguel began writing the most fantastical stories together."

Well, he supposed living without his memories was simply a different adventure. "I see."

"You will, in time," Joaquim said. "Now, let's get you packed up."

The plan was for him to retrieve his meager belongings from his rented room in the Barrio Alto and return with the others to the Golden City on the night train. As the Barrio Alto was a steep climb from this hotel, they needed to catch a cab for Joaquim's sake. Alejandro retrieved his shabby jacket from the back of his chair as Joaquim rose, and together they headed for the lobby to meet with Gaspar, who would accompany them.

Serafina waited there, though, too, as if she'd feared Alejandro would slip away.

"You don't need to come with us," Alejandro told her. "Why don't you get some rest?"

Her chin rose. "Do you think I'm one of those women who is constantly swooning? I don't need to rest. I want to help."

He nearly pointed out that she'd swooned the night before, but decided that wouldn't be wise. "I'd rather you not see where I've been living."

She looked stricken, as if for the first time realizing his life away from her might have been difficult. He had the impression his family was wealthy. He wasn't sure about Serafina's family, but neither she nor her father dressed like menial laborers.

"Please, let us handle this," he asked gently, taking her hands.

Tears glistened in her eyes. She glanced at Joaquim, as if asking reassurance that he wouldn't let Alejandro escape. "I'll go pack my own things."

Joaquim's hand settled on Alejandro's shoulder as he watched Serafina walk away, her slender shoulders slumped. "The last time you left her," Joaquim said, "they told her you died. I knew they were wrong, but even so, she was terrified and heartbroken."

And it must be hard for her to let him go.

Alejandro reminded himself to be patient.

On the fourth floor of the building, up a narrow old stairwell that twisted around, the flat wasn't much. There was a narrow bed with old, musty blankets that had once been blue, a small table with a single wooden chair, and little space to walk around those. There wasn't a toilet on this floor, so Alejandro had to make do with a chamber pot under the bed. He owned only two sets of work

clothing, but kept those neatly folded on the end of his bed.

At least he'd left it that way.

When he opened his door, he found his clothes and bedding strewn about. Gaspar entered first and walked about the small room, peering at each item, perhaps searching for magic. "It's safe."

Alejandro didn't feel safe, though. The three books he owned were torn apart. And thrust into the pillow was his knife, impaling a single piece of paper. "I didn't leave it this way."

"No," Joaquim said. "I didn't think you did. You've always been tidy."

Alejandro tucked away that thought—*I'm tidy*—and went to where a small painting of the crucifix hung on the wall. He lifted it down, popped the board out of the back of the frame, and withdrew a handful of mil-reis. "Whoever did this wasn't after my money."

"No, I don't think so," Joaquim said slowly as he removed the knife from the pillow and picked up the piece of paper there. It was a frontispiece from one of his now-ruined books, a decrepit copy of *The Mines of Solomon* he'd bought used in the market. Scrawled on the page were the words, *Don't talk.*

Alejandro peered at the sheet as he tucked his cash into a pocket. "That's idiotic. I can't remember anything to talk *about.*"

"Nothing recent?" Joaquim asked.

"I haven't been here long enough to make any enemies," Alejandro said with a shrug.

"This person was here last night," Gaspar said. "His contact with the knife has faded enough that I can tell it's been several hours."

Alejandro swallowed. If he hadn't spent the night in Serafina's bed, he might have ended up with that knife in *him* instead of in his pillow. Normally this would be his sign to move on, to find another city and start over again.

"Has this happened before?" Joaquim asked him.

His desire to flee was strong, but if he was going to trust anyone, it should be these two. He looked over at Joaquim. "Yes."

Chapter 2

Saturday, 18 June 1920, Lisboa

Serafina was waiting in the hotel's lobby when Alejandro returned, apparently expecting him to have retrieved a great deal of baggage. She glanced past him, arched brows drawn together. "I thought you went to pack."

"I did," he admitted, "but someone ruined what little I had." The intruder had ripped his clothes and destroyed his books. He and Joaquim had agreed there was no point bringing any of that back to the hotel, so all he retrieved was his money and his knife. "Joaquim says I have plenty of clothing back at his house, so I can just go there tomorrow."

Serafina held her hands close in front of her. Her dark eyes were worried. "What do you mean by _ruined?_"

Alejandro—he was actually feeling comfortable calling himself that now—gazed at this girl who was his wife. Was she the sort of woman who would handle the news well? Or would she become histrionic? His brief acquaintance with her suggested the latter. He took a deep breath and told her about the damage to his flat anyway.

She laid one hand over her mouth, her eyes wide and pained.

Alejandro took her hands in his. "Don't worry. It was just a threat."

"Has this happened before?" she asked.

She deserves the truth. He told her of the shadowy fear that had pursued him from France to Spain and now to Portugal. It always seemed like he would just get settled when he would feel the need to flee come over him.

Joaquim claimed that was his seer's gift, sending him forth ahead of his pursuer, although there was no way to know that for certain. *Something* had prompted him to go see Serafim Palmeira sing the previous night.

"So if you hadn't been with me last night. . . ?"

"That person would have found me there," Alejandro told her.

Her lips trembled, but she didn't cry, which was a relief to him. "Then it's a good thing we're leaving," she managed, lifting her chin. "I've canceled all my performances. We can go home and be safe there."

He kept hold of her hands. "Joaquim has said we can stay at his house for now, since it's larger than your parents' home."

She flushed. "Yes, I suppose that would be better."

"Joaquim also told me that . . . we never did have a wedding in the Church before."

Her eyes lifted, a line between her brows. "Do you . . . are you . . . going to leave me?"

He found himself blinking like an idiot. Had she been worried that he would? "Am I the sort of man who would abandon you?"

Her webbed fingers picked at his lapel. "You wanted to wait," she whispered, "and I was afraid you were changing your mind. I heard stories of what soldiers got up to in Angola, and . . ."

And so she'd convinced him somehow to marry her in order to hang on to him. Joaquim hadn't implied that, not exactly. "But you knew I would marry you eventually. Why not go ahead and do that now?"

"Are you sure?" she asked, tears glistening in her eyes.

What an awful question.

He didn't remember her. He didn't recall making any kind of promise to her.

If he was honest with himself, he was asking because he didn't want to see *himself* as the kind of man who wouldn't do what was right. He felt guilty that Old

Alejandro hadn't married her properly. Was he doing this only because he was expected to do so?

If he could have any woman in Portugal, though, he wanted Serafina. "I'm sure."

Her shoulders relaxed, as if she'd been holding herself tight.

Alejandro took her hands in his. "Now, we have to get ready for the train, but once we're underway, we can talk, all right?"

She gave him a glittering smile that set his heart at ease.

Alejandro kept his arms wrapped tightly about a sleeping Serafina as the train rattled through the mountains. The compartment's bed wasn't large, merely the bench pulled out and made up with blankets and sheets, but they would manage. The train shifted as they came around a wide curve, sending him rolling against Serafina's side.

They must be near Coimbra now. Even if he didn't remember Coimbra, he *could* read a map. Supposedly he'd attended the university there.

It didn't matter that everyone thought he was Alejandro Ferreira. He felt like an imposter. Would that ever go away? Or would he have to regain his memory to believe in this identity?

Serafina clearly believed. As did Joaquim and Inspector Gaspar and Marcos Davila.

He wanted to trust their judgment.

Serafina sighed and her arms twined around him. "Why are you awake?"

"Do you not worry that I'm an imposter?"

"I know you're not," she answered. "I don't need you to remember me to remember you myself."

Yes, this *was* a different experience for her. "Before," he asked, "what would we talk about?"

Her fingers touched his chest. "We only had three days. We didn't talk a great deal."

He had the impression now that they'd spent those three days in bed. "What did we plan to do? Live with my family forever?"

"We didn't discuss it." Her fingers wandered, informing him that *she* was the one who didn't like to talk.

He caught her errant hand. "We will have to talk about it someday."

"Can it not be tomorrow, then?" she asked. "I don't want to worry about little things."

Little things? Like where they would live? *I am clearly the practical one in this relationship.*

Sunday, 20 June 1920, The Golden City

The train station at São Bento he remembered. Not a real memory, but Alejandro had seen photographs of the intricate azulejos on the station's walls, tile murals depicting scenes from the country's history. He would have liked to stay and look at each one, but he could tell Joaquim wanted to get home, so they made their way out of the train station and called one of the cabs that waited there. It wasn't far to the house, Joaquim explained, but he would rather not walk, as the streets were steep. Alejandro suspected his brother had gotten less sleep on the train than he had, although not for the same reason, certainly.

And their destination *was* close, just a short drive down the main street before the station that connected the palace on its hilltop to the Douro River. This would be the Street of Flowers. The cab let them down in front of a dark stone house, one that looked like it belonged in the countryside, not the city. Joaquim opened up the wrought iron gate and proceeded through a small garden to the house. Carrying Serafina's two bags, Alejandro followed.

Nothing familiar.

Once they were all inside the long entryway hall and the door closed behind them, Alejandro spotted a petite woman hurrying down the stairs from the second floor to join them. Her hair was brown, and her eyes were dark and large. This was Marina, Joaquim's wife and the woman who'd raised him. She came running down the hall, threw her arms about her husband, and kissed his cheeks. Her clothes showed the same excellent taste as Joaquim's, a simple dress in dark blue. Even though she didn't need to work, she served on the board of the business firm her father ran.

She released her husband, turned to Alejandro, and held out her hands to take his. "Do you recognize me, Jandro?"

Her delicate features were pretty, and he suspected she was several years younger than her husband. He should *know* that sort of thing about his family, not just suspect it. "No, but you must be my mother."

She kissed his cheeks. "I am overjoyed that you're home. Joaquim kept promising me you would return someday, and I prayed he was right."

"I'm grateful for your prayers," he said, settling on what he hoped was a safe comment.

"And Serafina," she added, "Joaquim says you'll be staying with us for now, so why don't I have the footman take your bags up to your room."

A footman with a scar crossing his nose and one cheek came and whisked the bags away. Marina turned back to Alejandro. "Joaquim suggested we not give you too much to deal with at once, so the children are with their grandparents. They should be back in time for dinner, though, and will all want to talk to you then."

There were five, if he recalled correctly from his talk with Joaquim. "Could I see a photograph, to practice their names?"

"There's one in the sitting room." Marina slipped out of the hallway into that room and emerged with a silver-framed photograph of the family.

It had to be at least three years old, because *he* was in it, proof that he belonged here. He had some resemblance to the girls. The youngest child, the only boy, looked to be in a christening gown—likely the occasion for the photograph.

"I didn't know what was best," Marina added. "I'll leave the choice to you. Would you like to tour the house to see if it jogs your memory? Or perhaps just start with your room?"

"I would honestly appreciate the chance to change into clean clothes." He'd been feeling grubby since he'd walked through the front door. "Joaquim told me I still have clothing here."

"Yes, of course you do," Marina said. "And I know Joaquim would appreciate a nap. He never travels well. Perhaps a quick breakfast?"

"We had breakfast on the train, darling," Joaquim said.

"Oh, I forgot that. Then why don't you all go up and rest."

Alejandro made his way along the fine hallway with Serafina on his arm and headed up the stairs. "Which room is mine?" he whispered.

Serafina led him to a closed door only two away from the stairwell. It opened onto a large room that had recently been cleaned. It smelled of beeswax and freshly laundered linens. Alejandro stepped inside. A wide bed stood between two tall windows with iron-railed balconies outside. On the left side of the room, two doors led off into side chambers. A leather settee to one side of those doors had a stand next to it, with a coffee tray already waiting for them. This room made the one at the hotel look paltry. The burgundy bedding was finer than anything Alejandro recalled sleeping on before. This was a *prosperous* man's bedroom. He'd clearly underestimated the family's wealth. "Is Joaquim still in the police?"

"Yes."

That had to be a matter of choice, then. Joaquim surely didn't *need* to work, not given the grandeur of this house. He *chose* to.

Serafina dragged Alejandro toward one of the closed doors. "This is your dressing room."

The dressing room smelled a little stale, but Alejandro suspected that all he would have to do was request that the servants clean his garments, and they would. He crossed to an armoire and opened it to discover more jackets and trousers than he thought he would ever need. He wasn't accustomed to *choosing*. He took a deep breath. "What should I wear?"

"I'll pick it out for you." Serafina busied herself selecting a shirt and other garb, revealing that she had some familiarity with this room and his possessions.

"Did you live here while I was gone?" he asked cautiously.

Her hands stilled. "For a while," she said softly. "When they told us you were dead, I went back to live with my parents."

It was probably an awkward topic, but he risked it anyway. "Why didn't you stay?"

"I . . . Joaquim believed you would come back, but I wasn't sure."

He felt his brows drawing together. "But you knew I wasn't dead."

"I didn't think you were dead," she whispered. "I just . . . didn't think you wanted to come back. To me, I mean."

Alejandro found himself gaping. Serafina Palmeira—who was beautiful and a talented singer and would be any man's dream—wasn't sure her husband had loved her.

What exactly had happened between them during those three days? Apparently there hadn't been a great deal of talking, yet somehow she'd come out of that time with the impression that he would run from her.

He went to her side. "I'm back now."

She wrapped her arms around him and pressed her face against his tatty jacket. "Please let me stay."

He wanted to get to the base of whatever was bothering her, but he would need to do it delicately. He laid his cheek against her dark curls and prayed that he would figure out the right words that would keep him in this life. And her in it as well.

Meeting the children had been chaos. The girls wept over him. His nephew—too young to recall him—gave him a strange look, followed by a glance at his father, but then seemed to accept Alejandro's presence as inevitable. The children, on the whole, didn't seem to taken aback by the fact that he couldn't recall their favorite games or who had which room, but he *had* been absent for some time.

Serafina helped him, occasionally leaning close at the dinner table and whispering some fact into his ear. No one took his gaffes seriously, which was fortunate. They seemed inclined to be forgiving. Joaquim's wife seemed to struggle the most.

"I promised your mother I would never let you forget her," Marina said at one point. "I will have to tell you about her all over again."

Ah, now he understood Marina's worry. "I would appreciate that."

"She was an amazing woman," Marina said.

Joaquim had told him his mother had arranged to break all the sereia out of that far-away Spanish prison, and had suffered terribly in that quest. "Perhaps after breakfast tomorrow, we can talk."

Wednesday, 23 June 1920

That was the course for the next two days. He sat with Marina while she told him all about his mother and the conspiracy that had set her in a Spanish prison in the first place. He had long talks with Joaquim regarding his past. Inspector Gaspar came to speak with him about the hex laid on him. His cousin Rafael came to talk to Alejandro about being a seer, a talent that Rafael shared, and said that his sons would come to see Alejandro eventually. Alejandro met what seemed like scores of cousins and children, all of Serafina's sisters, and the Gaspar children. He listened endlessly, learning everything about Old Alejandro as if that man were a character in a play.

Flustered by all the names and relationships, he began making a chart to keep track. He did better once he'd written things down. It didn't help, though, that Joaquim and Duilio had married sisters, or that Duilio's widowed mother had married Joaquim's father—or rather the man who raised him. Nor did it help that they all seemed to have children to remember. Instead of a family tree, it made a family tangle. Fortunately, everyone proved willing to chatter endlessly about his family's past to help him figure it out.

The only person who *didn't* talk to him was Serafina.

So after meeting with Gaspar again on the third day, Alejandro went to find his wife. Unfortunately, she wasn't in their room, or the library, or the front sitting room. He asked the footman in the front of the house—Roberto, the one with the scar across his face—if he'd seen her.

"No, Lieutenant," Roberto said. "She said she was going to meet with her sister this morning. At a bookstore."

Alejandro felt his brows draw together. "Lieutenant? Did you serve in the war?"

Most of what Alejandro knew about that time had all come from a history of the Great War published the previous year by a Scotsman named Arthur Conan Doyle. Alejandro read it cover to cover, hoping the words would jog some memory.

"Yes, sir," the footman said. "In the Second Division."

That explained the scar. The Portuguese Second Division were posted on the front lines for eight months. After enduring a terrible winter, they were overrun when the Germans finally advanced on them. The Portuguese casualties had been high. "Did we ever meet?"

The footman shook his head. "No, sir. I heard you were in Angola for part of it."

"I was." Again, something he only knew from letters and that scar on his thigh. "Did you go straight to France?"

Roberto nodded. "Direct from training, sir. Then to Flanders. Wounded at La Lys and taken prisoner."

The Germans had taken a lot of prisoners that day. From letters he'd sent to Joaquim, Alejandro knew that he'd annoyed his superior officers by protesting the condition of the Second Division several times. He'd known a catastrophe waited in their future, and had hoped to change some part of it. Roberto was evidence that he hadn't succeeded. "But you've made a full recovery?"

Roberto rubbed a finger along the edge of his scar. It bore a hint of red along the edges, and pulled the outer corner of his eye downward. "My wife-to-be didn't want me back, not looking like this. I was lucky to find work in the city."

That reminded Alejandro how lucky *he* was. "I'm sorry to hear that."

One corner of the man's lips twisted, like a shrug. "The king himself came to talk to me in the hospital, sir. And the Duke of Coimbra visited there, too, though I didn't talk to him."

Alejandro was glad of that—that the country's nobility felt some responsibility toward the men they'd sent to war. "Someday I would love to speak with you about your time in Flanders, if you're comfortable with that."

"Mr. Mendosa said you don't remember any of it," Roberto said doubtfully.

The butler would have talked to all the servants to apprise them of his condition, to avoid any embarrassing situations. "No, I've never remembered anything."

Roberto shook his head. "Might be better that way, sir."

Wounded and taken prisoner, Roberto's experience had been far worse than his own. "Still," Alejandro said, "at some time when Mr. Mendosa wouldn't mind it, I would like to stand you a drink. Perhaps after hours?"

The footman seemed taken aback, but said, "If you'd like, sir."

Foiled in his efforts to find his wife, Alejandro headed back to his bedroom to puzzle over his life. One thing there might tell him about Alejandro Ferreira—a series of two dozen notebooks on a shelf in his armoire in the dressing room. He'd only peeked at one before.

The notebooks, examined more closely, were of varying ages. In the oldest, the handwriting was childish, while others displayed a more mature hand. He chose a pair of the oldest notebooks. He carried them to the tea table in the bedroom, flipped on the light, and sat down on the settee to read.

Eventually, Joaquim turned up at his bedroom door. "Are you coming down to eat?"

That means I've been reading for a couple of hours now. Surprised, Alejandro held out the notebook for Joaquim to see. "What did I copy this from, do you know, sir?"

Joaquim limped over and peered down at the pages. "Copy? What do you mean?"

"I've read it somewhere before," Alejandro explained. "I can recognize books I've read before, even if I don't recall when or where I read them." It was one of the stranger aspects of his memory loss. He could remember *fiction*, but not *reality*. Everything he'd read in this notebook so far was familiar.

Joaquim took the notebook, eyes narrowing. "Do you remember what happens in *this* story?"

Alejandro remembered most of the tale of a mother and son trying to get help to release the boy's father from prison. "The boy hits the man attacking his mother with a rock, and they escape to the nobleman's house—the father-in-law. His mother tries to threaten him with blackmail, but decides it would be wrong. The father-in-law is impressed with her honesty, though, so he vows to help her. They travel to Madrid, where he demands her husband's freedom."

Joaquim sat down on the end of the settee. "Have you read this book already?"

"That's what I was saying, sir," Alejandro pointed out.

Joaquim tapped the notebook with one finger. "No, I mean this notebook. *Today.* Have you read it through already?"

Alejandro shook his head. "No, but I recognized the story, so . . ."

Joaquim stared at him, mouth pursed as if he was trying to decide what to say.

"I don't understand," Alejandro said. "What's wrong?"

"You've wanted proof? This is your proof."

He stared at Joaquim for a moment, but found nothing to say. *How can this be proof?*

"Only Alejandro Ferreira would know how that story goes," Joaquim went on. "You didn't copy it. You *wrote* it, Alejandro, years ago. It's never been published, and I don't think anyone has ever read it other than myself and Marina—possibly Miguel—so you're *remembering* it."

Joaquim handed back the notebook. Alejandro touched its cover, almost reverently. There were more than twenty of these notebooks. "Did I write all of these?"

"Yes, and if you recognize the tales in them, that's because you recall writing them."

Alejandro threw his hands up. "Then why can't I remember Serafina? Or you?"

"I don't know," Joaquim said gently. "I'll ask Gaspar's opinion. But this is a step in the right direction."

Alejandro shook his head. He was tired of small steps.

After dinner, Serafina sat on the balcony in the twilight, her guitar in her hands. She played a mournful tune and, as Alejandro watched her, began to sing. It was the first time he'd heard her sing since that first night in Lisboa.

He simply watched her for a time.

He felt confident now that he wasn't an imposter. He *must* be the same man who'd written all those stories. That meant he wasn't doing anything illicit by bedding Serafina. It was a trivial thing to worry over, but it had bothered him since that first night, even though it clearly hadn't troubled her.

He wanted to get to know her. To understand her.

She had avoided being alone with him all evening, chattering gaily through dinner and then closeting herself with Marina to discuss wedding preparations. Alejandro suspected that as soon as he let her know he was there, Serafina would draw him toward the bed, and all thought of talking would flee. It *had* been a successful tactic so far.

She paused in the middle of her song, set the guitar aside, and jotted down a few notes. Her braid slipped over her shoulder as she leaned forward, ruining the illusion that she had short hair.

She's writing a song. He hadn't realized she wrote her own songs. He watched as she gazed down at the words on the paper, her lower lip caught between her sharp teeth.

Then she threw her hands in the air. "Where is Miguel when I need him?" she asked herself in a vexed voice.

Miguel? Alejandro stepped back into the shadows of the bedroom.

She rose, clutching the guitar in one hand, collected her papers, and came inside the bedroom before closing the balcony doors. It wasn't until she turned to lay the guitar on their bed that she realized he was there.

"Who is Miguel?" Jealousy roiled in the pit of Alejandro's stomach, an unfamiliar sensation.

She didn't start guiltily. "Your cousin," she said blankly. "Miguel Pinheiro. Have you not. . . ?"

Oh, that Miguel. "Why do you need *him*?"

Serafina looked puzzled—and a little hurt—by his tone. "To read my words. He always reads my poems."

Have I read any of her poems? Alejandro licked his lips, feeling that pit opening up at his feet once more, the feeling that he knew nothing about this wife of his. "May I read it?"

Serafina hesitated, a flush staining her cheeks. "You're not overly fond of poetry."

Am I not? Alejandro shook his head. It charmed him that she could be so shy about this subject when she was so forward on others. "I would like to read it. If you would let me, that is."

After a moment, she picked up the top sheet of paper and brought it to show him. "I've only just started this one," she told him. "I'm having trouble with the meter, matching it to the tune. I may have to rethink the notes to make them fit."

Alejandro angled the sheet of paper so he could better read the words written there in a fine, slanted hand. It was only half a poem, telling of a woman's loss of her lover, a topic Serafina knew better than she should at her age. Far too many Portuguese widows knew that loss. "It's lovely."

She stepped back, flushing. "Do you truly think so?"

Why did she doubt him at every turn? "Yes. It's unfinished, I can tell, but I think that once you've worked out the meter, it will make a lovely poem."

"I can't figure out how to end that fourth line," she said, gazing down at the paper.

The poem was arranged in quatrains, but he didn't know how to end that last line in a way that would keep the *spirit* of the words. He simply didn't know much about poetry—or music—and told her so.

"Miguel could figure it out," she said wistfully.

"Shall we go to see him? I haven't met him yet."

Serafina suddenly looked uncomfortable, her lips pressed together. "I, um . . . you quarreled with him."

So the fact that he hadn't met this particular cousin was *intentional*. He'd been to Rafael's house a couple of times now and had met the two younger sons, but not Miguel, the eldest. "What did we fight over?"

She shook her head, her eyes on the rug now. "He wouldn't tell me. He says you were a jackass, and he won't come around until you apologized."

Well, he'd known that sooner or later, *someone* wouldn't like him. He was perfectly willing to apologize, if only he could find out what he'd said. "Was it over you?" he asked his wife.

Serafina shrugged. "I don't know."

That meant it *could* have been his wife they were arguing over. "Well, I'll go over there and apologize tomorrow."

Her lips pursed in a way that suggested doubt. "If he'll see you."

Alejandro smiled down at her. "I'll be convincing."

Thursday, 24 June 1920

Alejandro's plan to seek out his cousin was set aside when another guest arrived at the house before breakfast, apparently bearing urgent news. One of the footmen knocked discreetly on the bedroom door just as Alejandro was drawing on his coat. "A gentleman has come to see you, sir," the young man said. "About your military service. I think he's someone important."

Alejandro cast a questioning glance at his wife, but she merely returned his look with her eyebrows raised. "I suppose you should go down," she said, picking up her cup of coffee again. She yawned and leaned back, tucking her scale-patterned feet under her on the leather settee. He'd learned quickly that she required a great deal of coffee in the morning.

Thus dismissed, he followed the footman down to the elegant front sitting room where Joaquim stood waiting with a stranger.

Or a stranger to me, I suppose.

"You don't remember me, Alejandro," the tall man said, "but Joaquim and I are old friends."

Alejandro nodded. He could tell that they were on good terms from the way they stood, no tension between them. The tall man had near-black hair, unmarked by gray, with a conspicuous widow's peak. Alejandro felt he should know that angular face. "I don't know your name, sir."

"Raimundo will suffice," the man told him. "Joaquim told me of the threat to you, and therefore I've made some inquiries with the military."

If only I could recall that face. He'd definitely seen this Raimundo before. Not before the war, but perhaps a photograph? "Were you in the military, sir?"

The man laughed shortly. "I'm afraid not. But I have some responsibility for what happened in France and Belgium. Why don't we all sit down?" Joaquim took his customary armchair and their guest sat on an old brocaded sofa, so Alejandro sat in one of the ivory chairs set across from it. "I'm here because I have some connections with the military," Raimundo clarified. "I had to go to Bastião to get this, Joaquim, and you're not going to like it."

"What did he find?" Joaquim asked.

Raimundo handed over a file. "I'll need to take that back with me, but I think there's time for you to read through it. Essentially, Alejandro was loaned to the British Expeditionary Forces, to their military intelligence people. Unfortunately, Bastião can't get any more than that. Whatever Alejandro was asked to do, the British want it hushed up."

Alejandro swallowed. "Have I done something terrible?"

"I don't think so," Joaquim said. "You signed this paperwork, Alejandro. I don't think you would have done so if you foreknew you would be asked to do something illegal, or that something bad would happen."

That was a complicated sentence. "Such as losing all my memories? How could I not have foreseen that?"

Joaquim set a hand on Alejandro's shoulder. "Because it's a question that would never occur to you to ask yourself. You were probably asking yourself whether you would have to break any laws or hurt an innocent. Or if you would be physically injured. Or more likely, if you would return home to your wife. Which you've done, so your gift would have reassured you that it was a safe chance. A seer has to ask himself the *right* questions."

Alejandro was beginning to think being a seer wasn't as wonderful a gift as it sounded. He pinched the bridge of his nose. "So I volunteered to work for British Intelligence. Why would they even want me?"

"I assume they needed a seer," Raimundo suggested.

"Does it say in my papers that I'm a seer?"

"No," Joaquim said. "There's no place in the paperwork for someone to list whether they're a witch. Just as there's no place to specify that you're not fully human."

That was why they'd returned the wrong body to the Ferreira family—none of his paperwork mentioned that his coloration wasn't human. "What happened to the body they sent to you? The man who wasn't me?"

"Since the army had no idea who he was," Joaquim answered, "we had him buried with military honors in a plot near our family's."

"If they mistook him for me," Alejandro said, "I'd bet he was involved in the same operation I was. Otherwise, why make that assumption?"

"Very likely," Raimundo agreed.

Someone he'd been working with had been burned so badly that only his feet were spared. Alejandro sat down, breath caught in his throat. "I've read that in a book before. A curse bounced back on him and . . ."

Raimundo gazed at him, dark brows drawn together as if to ask whether he was mad.

Joaquim set the folder aside. "Alejandro, tell me the rest of the story."

"Diamonds. They were supposed to steal something else—plans for an . . . assault—but they stole diamonds instead." If he closed his eyes, he could imagine them, trays of jewels, taken from a jeweler, ripe to be stolen *again*, because the Germans couldn't report them missing since they'd stolen them first. "No, the team stole both, but agreed to hide the diamonds and return for them later. Only one of them guessed that the . . . hero was going to turn them all in, so the other members of the team plotted to get rid of him before he could."

"What is he talking about?" Raimundo whispered, loud enough that Alejandro heard.

"Could I have written that?" Alejandro asked Joaquim. "Ahead of time, I mean."

"He recalls stories he wrote before," Joaquim said to Raimundo. "Gaspar thinks the hex on him only affects actual memories, but stories Alejandro wrote still exist inside his head because they're only stories."

"Stories?"

"He used to write adventure stories," Joaquim explained, "as soon as he learned to read and write. Some were quite fantastical, but many of the events in them were borrowed from real life."

"Could I have written one of my . . ." What was the word for it? He hadn't had visions, he'd simply known things. "Um . . . *foresights* . . . before I actually did those things?"

"I don't know." Joaquim pushed himself out of his armchair. "Let's find out."

Would there exist, among all those notebooks, the story of a Portuguese soldier asked to steal something for the British? Certainly enough seers had predicted the Great War. Joaquim led the way up to his bedroom, and gave Alejandro a moment to knock first to be sure Serafina wasn't in any state of undress.

She came to the door, her thick braid hanging down. Her guitar dangled from her webbed fingers.

"Darling, we need to look at the notebooks."

"Of course," she said, stepping aside. Then she saw that he and Joaquim weren't alone. Her eyes went wide, and she curtsied deeply to Raimundo. "Duke."

Alejandro turned an eye on Raimundo, and saw what he should have before. Not just a wealthy man, a man with power . . . but a man who had surrendered his power willingly to make the two Portugals into one. He *had* seen photographs of this man before. This was the former Prince of Northern Portugal, now the Duke of Coimbra, come to help a mere Portuguese soldier who'd lost his memory. "Sir? Have I offended. . . ?"

"It's fine, Alejandro," the duke said quickly with a dismissive wave of one hand. "I didn't expect you to remember who I am. That's why I'm here, after all."

"We're old friends," Joaquim offered. "And Raimundo knows I won't bend my knee to him."

Alejandro chewed his upper lip, but the duke seemed unoffended by Joaquim's lack of correctness.

"Why don't you come in and get the notebooks," Serafina said, looking uncharacteristically shy. She tried surreptitiously to pin up her braid.

Alejandro suppressed his smile. *All it takes is a former prince to quell her forwardness.* "Actually, I don't know which one I need. I've only read a couple."

"Why don't we take them all down to the library," Joaquim suggested. "We can sort them out there."

So they trooped into his bedroom and divided up the old notebooks. Serafina laid her guitar aside and joined them. Since Joaquim couldn't carry things downstairs—not and handle his cane at the same time—the duke ended up with a third of the pile, carrying them down the steps like a footman.

"What are we looking for?" Serafina asked when they'd set the books on the old round marquetry table in the library.

"A story about a theft where one of the participants is burned to death," he told her.

She shuddered delicately. "Like the man the army thought was you."

"Exactly. Or any mention of diamonds," he added. "If we all scan through these stories, we should be able to find it."

The talk of diamonds caught her attention, reminding Alejandro that he should purchase a new pair of earrings for her in lieu of a wedding ring.

"Sir, you don't need to stay," he said when the duke grabbed a handful of notebooks and settled at the table.

"Nonsense," the duke said. "Currently Ana is preparing our daughter to meet her soon-to-be husband. There are seamstresses there at all hours. I assure you, they don't need me."

If Alejandro recalled the newspaper stories correctly, the duke had only one child, a daughter who would marry the young heir to the Portuguese throne in Sintra, thus bringing the two halves of the House of Aviz back together and ending any question of the divided throne. "I appreciate your help, then, sir."

"You truly can call me Raimundo," the duke said, eyes on the pages before him.

Joaquim took another seat at the table and claimed a handful of the notebooks, while Serafina took one and settled on the couch. Alejandro gathered the remainder of the notebooks and sat in the armchair next to his wife. He loved this library with its musty smell and walls of old books. For a time it was silent in the room, until the duke sighed, got up, and rang for coffee. The butler popped his head into the room and dashed off to do the duke's bidding.

"You should get these published," the duke pronounced.

Alejandro realized that directive was aimed at him. "I think they need work, sir."

"I agree," he said. "However, the ones I've read are quite diverting."

"Half of them are autobiographical," Joaquim said, "and the other half are pure fancy. It's difficult to decide which is which at times."

"But still publishable," the duke said. "I have connections in that arena."

"You have connections everywhere," Joaquim replied blandly.

It was a tempting prospect, and might provide some income for him and Serafina. "I'll consider your suggestion, sir."

"Raimundo," the duke repeated.

Roberto came in then, bearing the coffee.

The duke glanced at the footman as he set the tray down on the table. "Are you one of our veterans?"

Roberto flushed, his scar turning red. "Yes, sir. I served in Flanders."

The duke rose and shook Roberto's hand. "I would love to speak with you after we finish here."

"Of course, sir." The footman bowed his way out of the room, apparently flustered by the attention.

Serafina poured for everyone. After a few minutes, they settled back to their reading. The room fell silent again save for the sound of turning pages and the occasional clatter of a cup in a saucer.

"I have it," the duke said after opening his third notebook. His dark eyes flicked across the pages as he began to read more thoroughly and they all waited expectantly on his verdict. "The hero of this story is named João, and he is, indeed, a common Portuguese soldier, caught up in an effort to steal some invasion plans from the German army."

He was flipping pages backward, as if to figure out how the story started. "Aha! The Englishman in charge saw João steal another soldier's wallet, apparently a jest of some sort. Since he needed keys stolen from a guard, he asked João because not only could he lift the keys, but he could also pass for a French civilian because he was fluent."

Alejandro licked his lips. Yes, he *remembered* that part of the story now. "Was there a Russian?"

The duke flipped through the pages. "Yes. The Englishman is actually Russian by birth and claims he's related to that dead madman, Rasputin." He glanced up. "When was this written?"

"There should be a date in the front of the notebook," Alejandro told him.

The duke looked and then regarded Alejandro with surprise. "1915. Rasputin didn't die until the end of the next year."

"The events in that story would have occurred in 1918, though," Joaquim noted.

"Impressive," the duke said. "You predicted Rasputin's death. In any case, why would the Englishman boast that he's related to a madman?"

"Because he was a witch," Alejandro recalled, "and having someone like that in your family makes you sound more threatening than you actually are."

"Is this the witch who curses João in the end?" Joaquim asked. "The Russian, I mean."

Alejandro tried to recall the story. "Yes, I think so."

Joaquim gave Alejandro a strange look. "A maledictor? That's a rare talent."

Alejandro had to bow to Joaquim's greater knowledge of witches—after all, he did work for the Special Police. "The man in the story specializes in cursing, if that's what it's called."

"Well what happened to them?" Serafina asked loudly, impatient with their digressions.

"They're sent to steal a battle plan," Alejandro said, finally recalling more of the details. "Behind the enemy lines in a town called . . . Lille. They were there for days hiding from the occupying forces before everything was right to make a move. João realizes after he does his part that the two who went inside stole *more* than the plans. They tell him and the Englishman that there were jewels, already stolen from a jeweler in town. If he keeps his mouth shut, they can divide the stones among themselves after the war . . . but João refuses to go along with it. One of the English tries to set him afire, but his effort rebounds on him and he dies instead, burned to death."

"Why?" Joaquim asked.

The duke squinted at the page. "Ah. Because João has an amulet given to him by an African witch doctor." He looked up. "Where would João have met a witch doctor?"

"An amulet?" Serafina asked, eyes wide. "Like an old piece of bone on a strip of leather?"

Alejandro blinked at her. "What?"

"Yes," the duke said. "It's described exactly that way in the story."

"You had one," Serafina said, bouncing in her seat like a little girl. "When you came back from Angola, you were wearing it about your neck. You told me some tribal leader gave it to you after you saved his son from a German bomb."

He felt idiotic for not knowing about an incident Serafina thought obvious. By now he should be accustomed to that. "German bomb?"

Joaquim answered. "An effort to sow discord between the Angolan troops and the Portuguese troops. The Germans planted bombs under several of the Angolan barracks, and then spread word that the Portuguese were responsible."

"Why would we ever do such a thing?" Alejandro protested. Even though Germany hadn't yet declared war against Portugal, the Portuguese had sent troops to their former colony in eastern Africa to help the Angolans protect their territory from the encroaching Germans.

"Some people don't need a great deal of urging to become angry," the duke said, "and there will always be those in our former colonies who blame us—*often with just cause*—for many ills they suffer."

Those sounded like the words of a man with a great deal of experience in diplomacy. "And I saved someone?"

Joaquim laughed. "You foresaw the incident and informed your commander ahead of time. At first they thought you were making it up. They didn't know you're a seer. But when they began to find the devices, they evacuated all the barracks before too many were hurt. Several men were injured, but no one died. One of the bombs wasn't caught in time, and you took a piece of shrapnel when you tried to hold back an Angolan soldier."

And that explained the wound to his thigh. "I see."

"I forgot to tell you that story," Joaquim said apologetically.

"Well, it's probably in these notebooks somewhere." Alejandro wished he hadn't been such a prolific writer as a young man. It would take him weeks to work through all these notebooks. "So I evidently was involved in an attempt to steal some battle plans, but became a casualty along with way because I didn't agree with their . . . additional theft. One of them tried to burn me to death, only to have the curse bounce back on him. I'm less inclined to inform the man's family now if we learn his identity."

"Even if he tried to kill you," Joaquim said gently, "his family would still want to know."

Alejandro sighed. Joaquim was a kinder man than he was.

The duke, who'd been reading all the while, lifted his head. "So the Russian curses you—I mean João—to forget everything, using the dead man's blood as the sacrifice, and he and the remaining man flee."

Alejandro pinched the bridge of his nose. "Wait. If I was incapacitated, how could I know they fled? So that I could put that in the story, I mean."

"This *is* a story," Joaquim said patiently. "Perhaps when you wrote it, you simply inserted the most logical conclusion."

It would have been better if he hadn't made things up. Now they couldn't be sure the man who'd cursed him was a Russian or that he'd even been involved in an effort to steal German battle plans. He might have been brought in to help steal someone's lunch menus. This wasn't evidence at all, and it didn't bring back his memories. "How does knowing this help us?"

"It gives me information to give to Bastião," the duke said, "something more to pry with. We know the approximate date, and now we have an idea what the operation was intended to do. With that he might be able to wheedle out the names of the others involved."

"And the one with a Russian name is the one who can take this curse off me," Alejandro said.

Serafina regarded Alejandro with knitted brows.

Joaquim's lips pursed as he thought that over. "True. I suspect the Russian isn't the one pursuing Alejandro, though. More likely to be the final member of the team."

The duke's brows pinched together. "Why do you say that?"

"Because the Russian would *know* whether or not his curse would hold. The person leaving notes for Alejandro seemed unaware that Alejandro still didn't remember who he was. He fears that Alejandro will tell someone where to find the missing stones."

Now they had an idea what the man threatening Alejandro wanted.

Diamonds. This was all about diamonds.

CHAPTER 3

Friday, 25 June 1920

Serafina had chosen the Café Elite for lunch that day, and Alejandro could guess why. Her younger sister, Mariona, had joined them, and after eating, the two suggested they might wander along Santa Catarina Street where the new café sat. The street was lined with shops and close to the Herminios department store.

Mariona sat with them now, sipping her coffee and trying hard to look sophisticated. Only eighteen, she was young enough to gape at the café's ornate Flemish mirrors, the plaster carvings of cupids and flowers, and the conservatory in the back. The newly opened café had been decorated in the Art Nouveau style and Alejandro didn't think he'd ever seen one more beautiful. He suspected it would soon become one of the city's most popular cafés, although he didn't care for the name. He didn't see himself as one of the *elite,* not after nearly two years spent digging sewers and laying paving stones.

Mariona whispered something into Serafina's ear, the two of them making a very vivid picture. Serafina's sister shared her fair skin and black hair, startling against the deep red velvet of the banquette on which they sat. And they were dressed nearly alike, Mariona in a stylish peach-colored dress, and Serafina in the same color but with an overlay of ivory lace.

Serafina smiled at whatever her sister said, her dark eyes laughing. "Mariona and I are going to visit the shops, if you don't mind. Can you find your way home alone?"

Serafina didn't realize it, but he wasn't alone. Now they knew the threat to Alejandro was more than just words scrawled on paper. Now they knew what someone didn't want him to talk about. There were diamonds involved, and people would kill for that. The footman Roberto sat at a table out on the street, close enough that he could keep an eye on Alejandro. Pressed into guard duty by the duke, Roberto had expressed his relief at the chance to spend a few afternoons beyond the butler's watchful eyes. And although Roberto hadn't trained for guard duty, he'd seen battle.

"I'll be fine," Alejandro told his wife. "You two enjoy yourselves."

Smiling, Serafina kissed his cheek and went on her way, Mariona in tow.

"I must say, she's every bit as pretty as you claimed," a voice said in English . . . with an English accent.

He knows me. No . . . he knows Old *Alejandro.*

Alejandro shifted to regard the man standing at his table. With blond hair slicked back from a rectangular face, he'd been distinctive enough that Alejandro had noticed him sitting on the far side of the café. The man's body language didn't betray any hostility, a good sign. "Why don't you join me?"

The Englishman settled on the velvet banquette Serafina had vacated. He crossed his legs, set his hat atop his knee, and regarded Alejandro with pale blue eyes that tilted up at the corners. "You neglected to mention the gills, though, Jandro. She's a *sereia.* You told me she trapped you into marrying her," he said. "Now I know how."

Had Serafina *trapped* him into marriage? Apparently he'd thought so, a strange thing since everyone had been aware he intended to marry her for years. Surely he hadn't simply volunteered that information to this man, not unless they were friends. Alejandro did his best not to let the man see any reaction. He didn't want the newcomer to know his needling had hit a soft spot.

"Personally," the man went on, "If *my* wife looked like that, I wouldn't care. Is the younger one unattached?"

"Not as far as you're concerned," Alejandro snapped automatically. "What do you want?"

"Of course, you don't remember me, Jandro," the other man said with a sad smile. "We knew each other back in the war."

You don't remember me. The certainty in the man's words said he knew the hex on Alejandro was holding. "You're the man who hexed me. I expected you to look more . . . Russian."

The man laughed dryly. "So Phillips has already gotten to you, has he? That lying prick."

And the other unknown man was named *Phillips*. "I haven't spoken with Phillips."

The blond man snorted. "No, I didn't expect Phillips to dirty his hands by finding you himself. How does one get a drink in this place? I'm parched." He waved over a waiter and placed an order in passable Portuguese.

"Why are *you* talking to me, then?" Alejandro asked.

"Phillips has been hunting me, you know," the man said. "He wants the stones. His henchmen have tried to kill me five times in the last four months. I must say, I'm getting rather tired of it."

What henchman would be stupid enough to try killing a witch who could curse him? *Most likely a henchman who doesn't know that fact.* "They haven't been successful so far, I see."

"No," the Englishman said, "but the government is tiring of cleaning up the mess when it happens."

The mess? Alejandro cringed. "What *have* you been doing to them?"

He opened up a silver case, offered a cigarette to Alejandro, and lit his with a match once Alejandro had duly refused. "The first four, I just stopped their hearts," he said, and blew out the match. "Not too difficult to pass off as bad men whose fate had caught up with him. The last one, though . . . I panicked and turned him inside out." He took a drag from his cigarette. "Right outside Whitehall, too, on Queen Mary's steps. Quite embarrassing, that incident."

Alejandro tried to picture what turning an assassin *inside out* would look like. It did not sound pleasant. "And how can I get you out of this mess?"

"We find the stones," he said with an elegant shrug, "and turn them over to the government. That'll pull Phillips' teeth."

Wouldn't this Phillips want recompense, then? Alejandro sat back as the waiter brought the man's coffee. Once the waiter had gone, he said, "You don't know where they are?"

"No," he said. "*You* hid them. The idea was that I would make you forget where, and after the war we would all meet back in France to retrieve them. Then of course, everything fell apart."

Alejandro felt his stomach sink. He'd actually gone through with hiding the stones? Had he been *complicit* in their plan after all? The story hadn't said that. "Ah."

"You don't recall what happened, of course," the man said, stirring his coffee with a little spoon. "When we met up outside Armentières, Lighter twigged you were going to snitch on him and Phillips, you being a good Catholic boy and all. He . . . well, he decided to stop you. I didn't realize what was happening in time to prevent it."

Lighter had to be the man who'd tried to burn him alive, the one whose corpse lay near the Ferreira family plot. Alejandro wasn't sure if that was a nickname or not, but it helped. "How would he find the stones, then?"

"He wasn't the brightest of sparks." He shook his head. "Didn't think that far ahead. For some reason, his flames bounced right off you and back onto him, charring him and leaving a rather gruesome and smelly corpse. Can you explain that part? I know you don't remember, but . . ."

"I was given an amulet," Alejandro told him, "by a witchdoctor whose grandson I'd saved in Angola. He said it would protect me."

"Apparently it did. Lighter fell on me—ruining my clothes, I must add. I panicked and threw the card I'd prepared at you, not realizing that I had a dying man's blood all over my hands." He stopped and took a drag from his cigarette, and then another sip of coffee as

Alejandro waited in silence. "The blood transformed my planned curse into a hex," he went on, "and was intense enough to physically knock you down. All three of us, actually. When I came to, Phillips was gone, and I had Lighter's blood all over me. God, not just blood. It was horrid. He was just lying there, all burned and stinking like a rabbit fallen into a fire. I thought *you* were dead."

Alejandro simply waited, watching the man's shaking fingers.

"With Lighter's blood and such all over me, I knew I would be the first suspected if the French police decided it was murder. I've been in similar situations before, so I fled. It took me a couple of days to figure out what had happened. From what I understand from the sanitarium, it wiped out *all* your memories. I never meant to do that to you, Ferreira. *Unintended* necromancy, yet I will probably burn in hell for it."

The man wasn't painting a particularly valiant picture of himself, which made Alejandro more inclined to believe him. "What *is* your name?"

"Markovich," he said, taking another sip of his coffee. "James Markovich. I'd forgotten what you people call coffee in this place. How do you drink this every day?"

The man probably preferred tea. "The Portuguese have fortitude," Alejandro said. "I'm surprised you arrived here so quickly."

Markovich shrugged. "Someone influential in your government contracted our intelligence people regarding you. They contacted my supervisor, who put me on a train then a steamer. Given that Phillips keeps an eye on me, I wouldn't be surprised if he's here too, already, planning to collect those diamonds."

"And how exactly do you expect me to help you find them? I don't remember any stones."

Markovich leaned closer. "Yes, but I can remove *part* of the curse. Not all of it, but enough that you might be able to tell me where you stashed them. Once we have them, we can draw Phillips out and take care of him once and for all."

Alejandro sipped his own coffee. Perhaps there was hope.

The police station on Boavista Avenue was under command of Captain Pinheiro—Alejandro's cousin, Rafael. In actuality, it was an old house converted into a station, with white-plastered walls and a tiled courtyard in the middle. It even had a small fountain, a very Andalusian touch. Alejandro rather liked that.

But they left the pretty courtyard and headed up the stairs to the offices, far plainer. Once there, Roberto settled in one corner, keeping his eye on Markovich, who wandered the office, surveying the wooden chairs doubtfully. Alejandro explained to Rafael the reason for the Englishman's presence. Once apprised, Rafael sent an officer off to find Inspector Gaspar and his wife. They arrived a moment later and firmly closed the door behind them.

A regal woman of mature years in a police uniform, the Lady sat down in a chair pulled out by her husband, who moved to stand behind her. Pinheiro leaned back against the door, arms folded over his broad chest, and Alejandro took a seat nearby. "This is Mrs. Gaspar," he explained to Markovich, "who is an expert on all manner of witchcraft."

Markovich glanced between the ivory-skinned lady in her police uniform and her part-African husband, then shrugged and wisely chose not to comment. "When did you acquire so many defenders, Ferreira?" he asked instead.

"I have a lot of family," Alejandro said. "Captain Pinheiro is my cousin, and I've always called Inspector Gaspar my uncle."

Markovich glanced doubtfully at Gaspar again.

Alejandro ignored the glance. "You work for the English government. Can't *they* stop Phillips?"

Markovich laughed bitterly. "He's been in Ireland. You may not know it, Jandro, but we've got a bit of a war on with the Irish. We're at a disadvantage on their soil."

Ah, yes. He'd read something about that. "Is he one of the separatists?"

"Yes. And those stones would go a long way in funding his cause."

That explained why this was happening *now*. "But why would Phillips try to kill you when I don't remember where the stones are?"

"Either way, he wins." Markovich finally chose a chair to sit in. "If he doesn't kill me, it prompts me to come find you to get the stones first."

"But if he kills you," Alejandro countered, "there's no way for me to remember where the stones are."

Markovich laughed shortly. "He believes that if I die, the curse on you will unravel."

"Reasonable," Mrs. Gaspar said. "Curses often fade in effectiveness as the witch loses interest in the victim, and can come apart after their death. This one, though, is a *hex*. They're horrible messy things, the bastard child of two different branches of magic, made of tangled entrails and thorny branches."

Markovich smiled at her admiringly. "I've not heard it worded that way before, Madame, but that's exactly how it felt coming out of me."

"Address me as Lady," she said softly, "or Mrs. Gaspar."

Markovich inclined his head as if to a queen. "As I suspect you know, I can't *fully* unravel the hex without resorting to necromancy again."

She smoothed her blue uniform skirt. "I thought that would be the case. I'd like you to lay out what you're going to try for me, first. And I want to observe your preparations."

Because they didn't want Markovich to make it worse, Alejandro realized.

Or turn me inside out.

He kept his mouth shut as Markovich and the Lady—with an occasional interjection by Gaspar—talked about the hex in obscure terms, sounding almost like surgeons discussing a patient's innards. Objects and intentions and talismans. Alejandro found his attention drifting.

He noted Roberto sitting silently in the corner, listening to everything with sharp fascination. As he'd been a farmer before the army, he was likely getting an education today. He'd had a few chances to chat with Roberto over the past few days. The young man had, like many, gone to war hoping to be a valiant soldier, a champion of Portugal. He'd wanted to have an adventure and win the admiration of his bride-to-be. Instead she'd been repulsed by his scar and refused to marry him. Roberto, however, firmly believed there was something better in his future, a woman who would love him and another cause for which he could fight.

Somehow, Alejandro believed that was true. If there was anything left of his seer's gift, he hoped it was telling him that Roberto's sacrifice wouldn't be for naught. He pinched the bridge of his nose.

Why did I write about the supposed theft of the plans, but not where I hid the diamonds?

"Lille," Markovich was saying, addressing Gaspar this time. "We were sent into Lille." Markovich retold the tale much as they already knew it from Alejandro's writings. They went through the steps of the theft and the team's quick flight afterward from Lille to Armentières.

"How did you get through the German line?" Gaspar asked to fill in one of the gaps.

"That was Phillips' job," Markovich explained. "Did I not say? He says he's part *fairy,* if you'll believe that sort of twaddle. Claims he used a glamour to hide us all from sight and we just walked out."

The Lady held up one hand to forestall her husband's comment. "You didn't believe him?"

"He's Irish," Markovich said with half a shrug. "They believe in fairy tales, you know."

One of the Lady's slender black brows quirked upward, but she didn't respond.

Alejandro shook his head. "Then how *do* you think Phillips accomplished his part?"

"He bribed the German outpost guards," Markovich said with a shrug. "Do you want me to believe he didn't pocket a single one of those diamonds before he came to meet us?"

That was always a possibility. Phillips and Lighter *had* been the ones to go into the German officer's quarters.

"And why haven't you tried to turn *him* inside out?" Alejandro asked.

Markovich shook his head. "That wily bastard won't meet with me, and everything I've tried from a distance doesn't affect him."

"You're limited to line of sight," the Lady observed with a tilt of her head.

"Yes, although it's better if I can make physical contact," Markovich said, turning back to her. "Else I would have cursed some German generals and gone home to England a lot sooner."

The Lady nodded slowly and, at a discreet gesture from her, Gaspar stepped forward to touch Markovich's arm. "They want to talk without you present," he said bluntly. "Come join me in the courtyard."

Markovich cast a glance in Alejandro's direction but rose and followed Gaspar out of the room. The Lady immediately turned to Rafael Pinheiro. "If he tries this, will it work?"

Rafael closed his eyes for a moment, talking with his gift. "Yes."

Alejandro hadn't believed until that moment. But Rafael was a seer, one who actually had his gift intact. This could work. He could regain his memories and his seer's gift with them.

"You understand that this borders on witchcraft?" the Lady asked.

"You're saying it will damn my soul?"

"No." Her head tilted toward the doorway out which Markovich had gone. "His might be in peril, though."

She was asking him to consider the man's soul. After he'd admitted to turning people inside out. "Do you think that's worth our concern?"

She shook her head in a worried fashion. "His gift makes him extremely dangerous, and I suspect he has few friends. He's a threat to them, always. One angry thought, a few words, and he can ruin someone . . ."

Like he did me.

". . . but you were clearly friends," she finished. "And that should matter to you."

He wanted so much to fit in with his family, his old life. His wife. Should he not try to reconnect with his old friends, even if they were like Markovich—pushy Englishmen? He thought again of his cousin Miguel, whom he'd not even managed to see yet.

He wanted his old life back, didn't he? But what would it cost Markovich? *And what might it cost me?* "I'll give it some thought."

The Lady rose gracefully. "Do so, Alejandro. I'll watch him make the removal talisman myself, but you're the one who will have to decide whether or not to use it."

Dinner that evening was solemn, as Alejandro explained to Joaquim and Marina their plan for the next day. He didn't need to ask where either of them stood on this issue. They didn't like the risk, but understood his desire to have his memories back.

Serafina kept her thoughts to herself. She spent much of the evening playing with the children. And later that night, once they were alone in their room, she distracted him from his questions in the way she usually did.

Afterward, Alejandro tried to catch his breath. Enough light came in through the window from a streetlight outside that he could see her features clearly. She laughed softly, and Alejandro felt his chest tighten. He stroked Serafina's curls back from her forehead. "I love you."

Her laughter fled. She turned her face away, toward the window.

His stomach went cold. No woman hated being told that, he would have thought. Not by her husband, at least. "Serafina, what is it?"

She sniffled. "You've never said that before."

He shifted on the bed and sat up halfway so he could see her face. "Never?"

She shook her head, still looking away from him. "All it took was your forgetting everything you knew about me."

"I would never have married you if I didn't love you, Serafina."

"You didn't have much choice, Jandro. I know that."

Was this why she'd been so uncertain about their relationship? Had she actually trapped him in some way, as Markovich had said?

"Serafina, look at me." He waited until she turned her head to gaze up at him, tears shining in her eyes. "Why would I marry you if I didn't want to do so?"

"After we lay together, you didn't have any choice." With a catch in her voice, she added, "And you didn't have much choice about that, to be honest."

Alejandro felt his brows rise. No choice about whether to lie with a beautiful young woman who was clearly in love with him? *Did she use her* call *on me?* Would that even work, since he was only half-human? "Why would you say that?"

She turned her head toward the window again. "When I came to the house that morning, I wanted to prove to you that I'd grown up, so . . ."

She would only have been sixteen or so when he left for Angola, while he'd been twenty-one. When he came back from Angola, she would have been eighteen. Grown up, indeed.

"How did you prove it?" He couldn't see her face, but her throat flushed. Her gills fluttered slightly, a sign of her agitation. He tried again. "What did you do?"

"You'll hate me for it," she whispered.

"I'm unlikely to hate you for *anything*, Serafina. I love you. I promise."

She remained silent for a moment. "I just . . . I waited until I knew your family would be gone to Mass, and I came to the house and to your room and . . . and you were still abed, so I . . . I joined you there." She finished on a whisper, as if that was too horrible to say aloud.

Alejandro sat back. "Why would I hate you for that, darling?"

She shifted to look at him, her dark brows rumpled. "You told me you weren't ready to marry. You had responsibilities. You were so angry with me."

Angry? And he hadn't recanted that sentiment during the three subsequent days he'd apparently spent in a hotel room with her?

What kind of jackass was I?

He'd told Markovich he'd felt trapped into marrying her.

And he could see now how it must have looked *to her*.

"Mother said you intended to marry me only because you foresaw it," she added, "not because you loved me."

He drew her back into his arms. Had he actually thought that? *Surely not.* "Tell me, darling. If I didn't want to marry you then, why not simply attend Mass with my family? I would have known you were coming to find me, wouldn't I? I could have locked my bedroom door, or arranged to be elsewhere. Instead I was there waiting for you."

That wasn't quite true. It was entirely possible for a seer *not* to know. He wasn't going to point that out, though. He was thoroughly annoyed with Old Alejandro. That Alejandro had agreed to marry her, but made her feel small and encroaching in the process. Had that been meanness on his part? Or had he simply been angry?

Serafina sniffled again. "I don't know . . ."

Alejandro took her webbed hand in his and kissed her knuckles. "Then let me be clear about it now. I love you Serafina, and I don't want you to forget that."

She made a sound halfway between a laugh and a sob, but then leaned up to kiss him, and soon they were no longer talking.

Saturday, 26 June, 1920

Joaquim met Alejandro in the library after breakfast. "I had the feeling you needed to talk."

Alejandro shut the library door and turned back to face his brother, the voice of sanity in the chaos of his life. "Did I love her? She doesn't think I did, you know."

Joaquim rubbed one hand down his face. "How do I answer that?"

"Truthfully, please."

Joaquim sat down on the couch and stretched out his bad leg. "You always looked after her. When you were younger, you saw her as a responsibility."

Alejandro leaned back against the library table and folded his arms across his chest. "You said I planned to marry her. Was that because I knew I would? *Only* because I knew I would?"

Joaquim closed his eyes, seeming pained. "When you left for Coimbra, Serafina was only thirteen. Between then and the day you married her, you only saw her for a handful of days out of any year. I don't know how you could have developed a mature love in that time."

In other words, Serafina had been right. Or her mother had, in that he'd married her only because he'd said he would. Because he'd predicted it. "That seems unkind of me."

"Marriages are often arranged with the two parties barely knowing one another," Joaquim said. "Love can grow from that. Look at Serafina's father and mother. Marcos and Safira had no choice, but they came to love each other deeply."

After Safira was imprisoned in Spain, Marcos had been kidnapped by his own grandmother and thrown in a cell with Safira. If that hadn't happened, Alejandro wouldn't have Serafina now.

Alejandro pinched the bridge of his nose. In a few hours, he was supposed to meet Markovich at the police station. When he regained his memory, would he be that former self again? Would he become that young man who wasn't considerate enough to tell his young wife that he loved her . . . even as he was in bed with her? If nothing else, he should have lied to spare Serafina's feelings. "Apparently Old Alejandro never even bothered to tell his wife he loved her," he admitted.

Joaquim's lips pressed closed as he thought through his response. "Did you tell her now?"

"Yes."

"Then you have a chance to set everything right with her."

Alejandro pushed himself away from the table. If he'd been a seer before, would he have foreseen that? Would he have seen losing his memory as a way to start over?

"Was she in love with someone else?" he asked. "With Miguel?"

Joaquim considered before answering. "My impression has always been that they are friends, brought together by family ties and a love of poetry. Perhaps you should ask one of them."

It would have been better if Joaquim had said no. Alejandro sighed. "Was I happy before? I don't mean about Serafina. I mean . . . in general."

Joaquim sat back and gazed at him. "I think you always felt responsible for everything. Rafael says seers often feel that way. They want to prevent every bad thing they foresee."

Joaquim was a seer as well; but, as Alejandro understood it, Joaquim's gift was very weak, subsumed by his finder's gift. Rafael was the powerful one. Even so, Rafael seemed content with his life.

"How does *he* deal with that?" Alejandro asked.

"He's trained not to take more on his shoulders than he can bear. He doesn't try to save the world. Even when you were young, that's what you were trying to do. You were always very serious."

"If I was that strong a seer, is it possible that I *allowed* myself to be hexed? Knowing I would be left like this? Without my gift? Or without access to it?"

Joaquim puffed out a breath. "I think that's a question only you can answer."

With Roberto guarding his back again, Alejandro made his way to the police station. Unfortunately, Rafael wasn't there to discuss Alejandro's questions about his gift. He was off chasing down a witch who'd left a large spell circle in a public square in Matosinhos during the previous night. A mystery, since no one had seen it done.

So instead Alejandro sat down between Gaspar and Roberto while Markovich prepared a talisman to remove the curse—the hex.

The Lady stood close by, watching every movement of the man's fingers. He clutched a Bible in one hand and lit a bunch of herbs. He let the smoke from them drift around a playing card he'd clamped into a stand, reciting verses in English. Alejandro vaguely recognized the words, but couldn't place them. Probably Psalms, given the cadence.

After a time, Alejandro decided Markovich was repeating himself. "What is he doing?" he asked Gaspar in a whisper.

"So far it looks benign to me. Protective. That's not the man's natural inclination, so it's not going to be terribly strong but . . . it might work."

Gaspar *saw* things. From what Alejandro understood, he sensed everything magical, like an added layer of sight or smell or sound. "So why the playing card?"

"The object doesn't truly matter," Gaspar answered. "It must have significance to *him*. That allows him to bind the curse to an object rather than passing the curse off via touch."

A trouble thought occurred to Alejandro. "Could he not have just sent me that in the post?"

Gaspar chuckled. "He still has to be in line of sight when it is . . . actualized."

"Why, sir?" Roberto asked, the first time he'd spoken.

"Limits. It keeps any of us from ruling the world," Gaspar said. "Me, I'm limited to seeing what is, not what can be. As a seer, Alejandro is limited by his guilt. If ever a seer is born without a conscience, we would all be doomed."

"Guilt over what?" Roberto asked, thick brows drawn together.

"Guilt over what he can and cannot prevent. A seer must continually balance whether an action will result in harm to someone else. Sometimes that guilt is overwhelming. Sometimes they decide who lives and who dies."

Roberto turned his gaze on Alejandro. "You went to Flanders to prevent the battle, didn't you?"

That had been behind all the letters he'd apparently written to politicians. Behind his numerous complaints to superior officers about the Second Division's ragged state. He'd *failed*, and people like Roberto had paid the price for his failure. He felt sick to his stomach.

It seemed like the entire world flared into sharp detail around Alejandro. The hiss and pop of the burning herbs, their heady scent, the words that Markovich clicked off in English, far more guttural than Portuguese. "I don't want to do this."

Laying one hand on Markovich's arm, Mrs. Gaspar regarded Alejandro with one slender eyebrow quirked upward. "Your concerns?"

"I don't want to remember," Alejandro admitted.

Markovich dropped the burning bundle of herbs on the tiled floor and stomped on it. "I've come a long way to end this, Ferreira."

The air in the room suddenly felt scorched, dry in his lungs. Alejandro held his breath.

Gaspar faced the Englishman. "Are you threatening him? We already have your confession that you hexed him. I have enough to turn you over to our government at this point. And don't think you can curse *me*, English."

That was why Gaspar was here rather than Joaquim—Gaspar was immune to magic. And Markovich couldn't curse the Lady either, since she wasn't entirely human. Any curse he laid on her would apparently go awry. Roberto was at risk, though. Alejandro rose and put himself between the footman and Markovich.

Markovich's attention was on Gaspar, though. In a peeved tone, jaw clenching, Markovich asked, "Want to try it, old man?"

Gaspar folded his arms across his chest.

"He's valuable to the English government, Uncle," Alejandro said. *A maledictor would be, to any government.*

Of course, Gaspar knew that. He was merely trying to get a reaction out of Markovich.

But Alejandro knew now why he'd let Markovich hex him, why he'd been there in the wrong place at the wrong time. Or, for his purposes . . . the right place and the right time.

He'd wanted his gift gone, his memories gone. *This was completely voluntary.*

Because he couldn't live with the anguish of being unable to stop the Battle of La Lys, the hundreds of Portuguese dead, the thousands taken prisoner.

He'd been able to change events in Angola, stopping the bombings of the Angolan barracks and saving lives there. He'd made a difference.

But he hadn't been able to stop La Lys.

Rafael and Joaquim and Duilio hadn't either.

None of the seers of the Jesuit brotherhood in Lisboa had.

Alejandro got to his feet. "Anything else I can do to help you, I will," he told the Englishman, throat tight, "but I don't want to be the man I was before."

Markovich grabbed the card out of its wire holder and threw it onto the floor. He took a quick breath, almost spoke, and slapped a hand over his mouth.

Gaspar jumped in front of Alejandro. "Hold your tongue, man!"

Too late. Alejandro felt his guts twitch as Markovich visibly struggled to control his anger, his shoulders hunched and his hand clamped over his mouth. But sounds still leaked past his fingers as if they had a life of their own. Alejandro fell to his knees, his innards suddenly afire, and retched up what little breakfast he'd had.

CHAPTER 4

_____

Saturday, 26 June 1920

ALEJANDRO CLUTCHED his gut in agony but, as abruptly as it had begun, the twisting of his innards ceased. For a moment he lay there, disbelieving. Then he worked himself onto his hands and knees and gasped in air as the others clamored around him. Sweat dripped from his hair, stinging his eyes as he looked up.

The Lady stood between him and Markovich, her hands held wide. She was blocking the curse by creating a glamour and making Alejandro unseen. *Line of sight.*

Her husband stood behind her, a second, *physical* block since Gaspar was immune to magic.

Alejandro coughed. They had put themselves between him and the curse. They'd defeated a maledictor. "You stopped him."

The Lady glanced down at him. "To be honest, I've no idea if that would have worked," she said, pointing, "but that did."

Past her skirts, Alejandro saw Markovich lying on the ground unconscious. Roberto stood over him, rubbing the reddened knuckles of one hand in the other, jaw clenched in fury.

Alejandro coughed, then lay back on the floor and thanked God he wasn't inside out. "Thanks, Roberto," he croaked.

Isabella Anjos held one hand to Alejandro's throat, her eyes closed. The pretty young woman was only sixteen or seventeen, with dark blond hair worn cropped short in the current fashion. Her uniform reminded him of a novice at a monastery, but instead of black, the dress under the white apron was the blue of the Special Police. That she was a healer explained her tutelage here under the senior healers gathered at the military hospital across the street from the Special Police's station. It kept the healers both within easy reach of the Special Police, and at a hospital where they might aid the doctors.

Inspector Gaspar had dragged Markovich to a hospital room there until the Englishman should regain consciousness. He'd ordered Alejandro to find the healers . . . just to make certain Markovich hadn't done anything *permanent* to him. Upon spotting him, Mrs. Pinheiro—his cousin Rafael's wife—directed him to a small whitewashed room and ordered him to wait while she fetched in her pupil.

Apparently Alejandro knew the girl. Her parents too, although they'd both died during the Great War. Given the warning look Mrs. Pinheiro cast his way, he didn't ask *how* or *where*. That was the sort of question one asked another soldier or a close friend, not an orphaned child.

After a short time, the girl opened her eyes and lifted her hand from Alejandro's throat. "You'll be fine, Mr. Ferreira."

Evidently they weren't friendly enough for her to use his given name as everyone else did.

No matter what this girl said, his head hurt and his guts felt unsettled. "Thank you," he said anyway.

She rose from her bedside chair and gazed down at him, dislike now apparent in the hard set of her delicate jaw. "Why haven't you gone to see Miguel?"

Mrs. Pinheiro took a breath and appeared ready to intervene, but then changed her mind. Perhaps she wanted that answer as well. She was, after all, Miguel's mother.

Alejandro gazed up at Miss Anjos. "I can't remember. I don't know what he and I fought about."

"So I hear," she said in a dry voice. Her hand balled into a fist.

"Isabella," Mrs. Pinheiro said softly, "control."

The fist at the girl's side slackened, but Alejandro didn't make the mistake of thinking she was in charity with him. "Whatever happened between Miguel and me, Miss Anjos, I'm willing to atone for it. I am sorry that we fought, even though I do not know why."

"You called him a *cripple*! How dared you say such a thing?"

Alejandro found himself blinking in a stupid fashion. *Why would I have. . . ?*

Mrs. Pinheiro set a hand on the girl's shoulder. "Would Miguel appreciate your interference, Isabella?"

The girl's jaw firmed again, her glare never lifting from Alejandro. "No."

Mrs. Pinheiro's intercession had given Alejandro time to gather his thoughts. "I've been meaning to come to your house to talk to him," he said quickly, "only I've been distracted by that Englishman for the last couple of days."

"He has his own flat," Mrs. Pinheiro said. "It wouldn't be appropriate for Miguel to live with us while Isabella is doing so."

The Pinheiros had three sons, all adopted, if Alejandro recalled his family chart correctly. While Miguel was close in age to Alejandro, the two younger ones would be near Isabella's age. If they could be trusted around her but Miguel couldn't, there must be something between the two of them.

"No one has mentioned to me that he doesn't live at your house," Alejandro clarified. "Not even my wife. That explains why I haven't seen him there when I've gone to meet with your husband."

Mrs. Pinheiro tapped Isabella on the shoulder. "Why don't you go back to Miss Prieto now?"

Isabella obeyed, straight nose in the air, not bothering to take her leave of Alejandro. That left him alone with Miguel's mother.

"Miguel's going to make it difficult for you," she told him. "You know how he is."

"No, I don't," he told her, sounding plaintive even to his own ears. "That's the problem. Why would I have said such a thing to him?"

His cousin's wife settled gracefully in the chair Isabella had abandoned. "I suppose you've had too many things to catch up on. When he was six, Miguel was run over by a carriage just outside this hospital, which is why he was brought to us at all. One of the military doctors had the gall to suggest we should let the boy die. That's never a wise thing to say to a handful of healers."

He found himself laughing softly. "I suppose you saw it as a challenge."

"We all did," she said. "In time, most of his injuries healed, but his lower leg was shattered. We couldn't fix that completely—not the bones. Most of the time a cane suffices, but when it's paining him he requires a crutch. Miguel is prickly about that. Whatever you said to him must have hurt his pride."

"I will do my best to make it up to him. I am beginning to believe that the Alejandro of before wasn't the best of friends or husbands," he admitted, something he hadn't said aloud to anyone but Joaquim.

She smiled gently. "Just be prepared. I don't know where he got it from, but Miguel's ability to hold a grudge is unequalled in all of Portugal."

Well, at least it isn't all of Iberia. Alejandro took his leave of her and made his way over to the other hospital room where Markovich waited with both Roberto and Inspector Gaspar playing watchdog. Markovich lay on the bed, fully dressed, but struggled to sit up when Alejandro entered. He held a towel-wrapped item to a jaw that was already swelling.

"I'm sorry, Jandro," he said. "I didn't mean to . . . well, you know." He waved his hand vaguely in the direction of Alejandro's gut as he said that.

Alejandro had to make an effort not to flinch away from that casual gesture. "We'll just need to find another way," he said. "I'll start looking through my notebooks and see if I wrote it down there."

Markovich rolled his eyes and fell back against the pillows with a melodramatic groan.

One of Gaspar's brows rose. "Haven't you already looked?"

"I have, but there has to be something written down somewhere. I'll find it." He felt strangely sure of that as he spoke. Perhaps it was his seer's gift, lurking under the hex yet still present. "We'll pull Phillips' teeth," he told Markovich. "I'll find a way."

Markovich heaved another heavy sigh and turned to Gaspar. "Am I under arrest or not?"

Gaspar shook his head, and Markovich shoved himself off the bed, dropping the wrapped bit of ice on the cover. He left in a huff, promising to return to his hotel to wait for news. Alejandro didn't care much where the man went just now, as long as he was out of sight. Or rather, as long as Alejandro himself was out of the man's line of sight.

"Since you've decided not to attempt removing the hex," Gaspar asked, rising, "do you have another plan of action?"

He had no idea where to look yet. But there was one problem he *could* fix. "Do you happen to have Miguel Pinheiro's address? I want to go visit him."

Roberto opened his mouth, but swallowed his comment.

Gaspar's brows rose, both this time. "Is that important just now?"

"It's important to my wife," Alejandro said. "And everyone in the family, I suppose. I don't want a cousin as my enemy."

Gaspar shrugged.

"And I feel like I need to do it," Alejandro added. "I don't know if that's my gift or just guilt, but I feel like this will help with . . . everything else."

That brought a rare smile to Gaspar's face. "I don't know his address, but I can find it on Rafael's desk."

Like most buildings in this part of the Golden City, the houses were packed together like sardines in a tin, long and narrow flats on each floor. The old stone was musty, and the plaster on the walls needed work. And for a man who used a cane, climbing three flights of stairs daily must be difficult. Alejandro heaved himself up the creaking steps of the old house to the fourth floor, his gut still twisting. Roberto had joked about catching him if he fainted and tumbled back down the steps. Alejandro didn't entirely dismiss that possibility.

He stood for a moment in front of Miguel's door. *What should I say?*

There was honestly only one thing to say. He squared his shoulders, knocked on the door, and waited. He glanced at Roberto, who shrugged. But then he heard steps inside the apartment and the door opened.

The young man who looked out at him surprised him. Miguel Pinheiro was tall and everything about him was lean. Even his face was narrow, his straight dark hair a touch overlong, his eyes almost black. He looked nothing like his father, a reminder to Alejandro that Miguel and his brothers had been adopted. In a deep voice, he rumbled, "What do you want, Jandro?"

"I came to speak with you," he said, very aware that he hadn't been invited inside. "To apologize."

"And you had to bring Mr. Machado as your reinforcement? I don't have time for this," Miguel said, and shut the door in Alejandro's face.

Alejandro blinked at the sight of the closed door, taken aback. It took him a moment longer to realize that Machado was Roberto's surname; he'd never bothered to ask. He felt a flush creep along his cheeks. Miguel had managed to prove that Alejandro didn't know his own household as well as he did. It was also telling that Alejandro hadn't bothered to learn the name of the man who might have saved his life an hour before. "I'm sorry, Roberto. I may have wasted your time."

Roberto leaned against the narrow hallway's peeling wall. "You're here, sir. You walked up all those steps. Might as well try again."

Alejandro knocked again, more forcefully this time. "I'm not going away," he yelled into the door.

It only took a few seconds this time. Miguel opened the door again, lips pressed in an annoyed line. "Leave me alone, Jandro."

"I can't," Alejandro said. "My wife needs you to look at some of her poetry, and she doesn't want to go around my back to see you."

That seemed to surprise Miguel. "And you expect me to believe you care what she wants?"

Alejandro swallowed a defensive retort. *I deserve that. Old Alejandro deserved that.* He took a careful breath, and said, "I am *trying*, Miguel. I want her to be happy."

Miguel's eyes narrowed, staying on his for a moment, then he stepped back—limping noticeably—and held the door open. "You'd better come in, then."

Alejandro followed his cousin inside, Roberto behind him.

It was a cluttered place, one of a man who loved his books. There were books piled on every table, on a set of rickety looking shelves next to the window, stacked on the floor behind the door. Slips of paper marked pages within many of them. A wide wooden desk set under the front windows held a typewriter and a neat sheaf of blank papers, files, a magnifying glass, and several newspapers. Miguel's jacket hung off the back of the wooden chair.

"Are you working on a new article?" Roberto asked in a friendly tone.

"Always," Miguel told him with a self-deprecating shrug.

"He interviewed me for one of his articles," Roberto said to Alejandro, "about men returned from the war having trouble finding work."

So not only did Miguel write poetry, but he wrote for the newspapers as well. Important articles, like the difficulties of veterans. Alejandro was impressed. "Which paper do you write for?"

The gaze Miguel turned on him was markedly cooler than his friendly expression toward Roberto. "Whichever will publish a cripple's work."

So his mother was right—a grudge as wide as Portugal. "Miguel, whatever it was I said, I know it was offensive. I don't know how I can apologize for something I don't recall, but I am sorry we're no longer friends because of it."

Miguel continued to glare at him.

Alejandro sighed. "Surely you've heard by now that I don't remember anything."

"Yes, I've heard."

But he didn't believe it. "I truly can't remember whatever it was I'm apologizing for. I know that Old

Alejandro was a horse's ass, but I can't recall the specific sin here. Tell me what I said, and I'll beg your forgiveness, but otherwise I can't."

Miguel jaw clenched. "You said I should be grateful I'm a cripple so I wouldn't be sent to war for my king."

Alejandro felt his mouth fall open, and couldn't seem to close it for a second.

I hope I was drunk when I said that.

He could grasp exactly how those words had come out of his mouth. Or rather, Old Alejandro's mouth. If he'd foreseen the conditions in Belgium, if he'd foreseen that terrible battle, he might have said just those words. It was possible that he hadn't meant it as a reflection on his cousin.

Miguel would only have heard the words, *You're a cripple.*

He'd probably heard it as an insult to his bravery, a belittling of his desire to serve his country. He might have heard it as an insult to his manhood. He would have heard it as a statement that he wasn't Old Alejandro's equal. And even if Alejandro had forgotten saying that, Miguel never would. He'd clearly shared it with Miss Anjos.

Alejandro cursed under his breath, grateful that Miguel hadn't repeated those words to Serafina. "I do apologize, Miguel. I . . ."

Miguel waited.

"I am trying not to be the person I was before," Alejandro said. "I am trying to be a better husband, a better friend. I'm sorry that it's come so late."

Miguel frowned. "You thought you were the center of the world, before."

Joaquim had told him that, although not in such damning terms. Joaquim had phrased it in terms of responsibility. "I gather that humility wasn't one of my virtues."

Miguel let out a short bark of laughter. "God, no."

"I'm working on it, Miguel," he said. "I am trying. For Serafina's sake can we try to be friends? It's important to her. She wants your insight on her work, but feels like she can't ask while we're estranged."

Miguel shook his head, but after a moment, asked, "So she's writing again?"

"Yes," Alejandro admitted, taking hope in the change of topic. "What I've read seems very good, but I'm not a judge of poetry. She thinks you would be able to advise her."

Miguel touched one of the files on his desk. "I can do that, I suppose."

"Could you come for dinner some night this week?" Alejandro asked. "Or next week?"

"Do I take it that you're reconciled to being married to her now?"

So Miguel was offended for Serafina as well. "I don't know what Old Alejandro thought, but I'm very fortunate," he said. "She's talented and lovely, and I don't deserve her."

Miguel looked over at Roberto, as if for reassurance, then turned back to Alejandro. "No, you don't, cousin."

An uncomfortable silence followed, and Alejandro had no doubt now that Miguel had fancied Serafina at some point, no matter what he intended toward Miss Anjos now. He could easily understand that, given their mutual interest in poetry.

Breaking the silence, Miguel nodded toward a bottle of Vinho Verde sitting on a bureau across from his desk and asked, "Would you like a glass?"

Alejandro hadn't had dinner, but he wasn't going to turn down what seemed like an olive branch from his cousin. "Yes."

Miguel opened the bottle and poured three glasses. He handed one to Alejandro and one to Roberto before picking up the third. "To Serafina," he said, raising his glass.

They joined him in his toast. The wine, more potent than Alejandro expected, went to his head quickly.

An hour later, all three of them sat on the floor, apparently believing that was necessary.

Alejandro stared down into his empty glass. At one point, Miguel had threatened to take a swing at him, and

Roberto intervened. Now the footman-cum-bodyguard sat between them, a solid buffer. It was their third bottle. Or perhaps their fourth.

"And you were shit to her before you went to France," Miguel was saying.

Alejandro was fairly certain they'd covered that ground three times already. Or perhaps four, once per bottle. "I know, Miguel. I'm sorry."

"You feel bad now," Miguel said, "but you'll go back to being a horse's ass soon enough."

He didn't want to do that.

"He doesn't want his memory back," Roberto told Miguel. "Doesn't want his powers back."

Miguel shook his head blearily. "No."

"It's true," Roberto said, rubbing a hand along the scar that lined his face. "If I could forget the war, I would, too. I hate the English, leaving us out there to die on the front line like that. I wanted to be valiant, but we had no chance against so many Germans."

"You'll have your chance," Miguel answered. "Remember, I told you."

For a moment, there was silence. Alejandro felt like he'd missed something.

"I did annoy the English," Roberto said then. "I was never more pleased to hit someone."

"What are you talking about?" Miguel asked.

Roberto blinked at him owlishly. "The English fellow, the witch who tried to curse Jandro's insides out."

"You're lucky he didn't curse *you*," Alejandro said.

"I listen," Roberto said, puffing up. "Came up behind him. He never saw me."

"Oh," Alejandro noted. *Line of sight.* "Smart of you."

"What are you talking about?" Miguel asked again, louder this time.

"He wants me to find some diamonds," Alejandro explained, "but I don't know where they are anymore."

Miguel leaned forward to regard Alejandro with exaggerated seriousness. "Like in that story? Where you mailed a sack of diamonds to the Holy Sisters?"

A fierce pounding on the door made them all start guiltily. "Alejandro, I know you're in there," Gaspar called. "We need to talk to you."

Recognizing the seriousness in Gaspar's voice, Alejandro pushed himself to his feet. He crossed to the door and, grasping the doorframe to steady himself, threw it open.

Inspector Gaspar stood outside, his dark face grim. "Serafina's missing."

Joaquim scooted over in the large Ferreira coach, making room for Miguel and Alejandro to sit across from him and Gaspar. "When your wife didn't return from her afternoon at her parent's house, Marina became concerned. She sent a footman to check with Serafina's parents, and they said she'd left over an hour past."

God, no. Phillips or his henchman had to have grabbed her in a twisted attempt to get Alejandro to help him find his diamonds.

"Can you *find* her?" Alejandro asked through the fog in his brain. That was Joaquim's special gift—he could find people if he knew them or if he could touch something of hers.

"I'm having trouble," Joaquim said. "I get a brief glimpse of her, but nothing more. That tells me she's being hidden."

"Hidden?" Miguel asked, rubbing a weary hand down his face. "How?"

"According to Markovich—the Englishman," Alejandro explained for Miguel's sake, "our Irish associate is half fairy."

"So he can cast a glamour around her?" Miguel asked. "Like Mrs. Gaspar does?"

Gaspar, sitting across from them, held onto the hand strap as the coach made a turn. "That's my guess. If Joaquim is sensing her at all, that means either Phillips doesn't control his glamour as well as he'd like, or . . ."

"Who is Phillips?" Miguel asked, massaging his forehead now.

"The Irishman," Alejandro said.

Miguel shook his head and then grimaced. "Wait, is this still the story with the diamonds? With the Irishman and the Russian?"

In the evening light that filtered into the cab, Gaspar fixed Miguel with an intense gaze. "What are you talking about?"

"He's read that story, Uncle," Alejandro said.

"I used to read through Jandro's stories for him," Miguel said waving one hand as he spoke. "Edit them. I still have a bunch of his older ones in my files."

Gaspar's brows rose. "The story I read didn't mention an Irishman."

Alejandro puzzled at that.

"There wasn't an Irishman," Joaquim agreed. "Not in what we read."

Miguel groaned. "No, it's the version Jandro left with me. He made changes to it and left the most recent version with me before he went to Angola. I have that notebook . . . somewhere."

The driver made another sharp turn. His stomach lurching, Alejandro asked, "Where are we going?"

"Matosinhos," Joaquim said. "When I do get a flash of Serafina's location, it's in that direction."

"And combined with Rafael's encountering a fairy seeming there this morning, I suspect that's where our half-fairy is."

Alejandro wondered if he'd missed something or if he was just drunk. "A fairy seeming?"

"It looked like a spell circle, so someone sent for the Special Police. That's what Rafael was off doing while you were with Markovich this morning. It was a diversion, I suspect, or a way to see who would respond."

Alejandro shook his head. He'd wanted to talk to Rafael, but he hadn't been at the police station. Had that only been this morning?

"The seeming was already fading away by the time Rafael got there, but he had a feeling about that place," Joaquim went on. "He's currently gathering up Markovich. They'll meet us there."

Alejandro hoped he didn't cast up his lunch on the way. Between what Markovich had done to him, the coach's rattling over the cobbles, too much wine on an empty stomach—and worry—he was queasy. What was happening to his wife right now? Had Phillips hurt her? He pressed the back of his fist to his mouth.

"Have faith," Gaspar said. "He needs her to negotiate for the stones."

"I don't have his damned diamonds," Alejandro pointed out. "And I don't have any idea how to get them back."

"You mailed them to the Holy Sisters," Miguel said, eyes squinted shut. "In . . . some town that had beer."

"Every town has beer," Gaspar said.

Joaquim turned a sharp gaze on Miguel. "Is that in the version you read, Miguel?"

Miguel was thinking hard, mouth pressed into a grim line. "João gave them to the mail-girl to post, then warned her to leave Armentières immediately because the Germans were about to invade. She wrote the address on the package because João didn't know it . . ."

João was the name of the main character in that story, Alejandro recalled. The name he'd taken after leaving France.

"Popper . . . *something* . . . was the name of the town," Miguel added.

"Poperinge?" Gaspar asked.

"That's it," Miguel said and snapped his fingers. "The Church of Saint John, for the war orphans."

An orphanage. He'd sent the diamonds to a church orphanage.

Alejandro crossed himself as a thousand pounds of guilt lifted from his shoulders. It didn't help him to get Serafina back, but he silently begged God to be merciful because Old Alejandro had *tried* to make something good out of a bad situation.

Did I know before that Serafina would be taken as a result of my actions? That she would be endangered? Surely if he'd foreknown that, Old Alejandro wouldn't have chosen this path.

But it didn't matter what Old Alejandro had known . . . only what *he* was going to do now. Alejandro opened his eyes. "Did Rafael say anything? About whether we'll get her back safely?"

Miguel hit Alejandro's leg with a fist. "Don't tempt fate."

"I need to know," Alejandro hissed at him.

"Rafael said it wasn't up to us," Joaquim said softly, "so he couldn't answer."

Alejandro blinked at his older brother, appalled. "What does that mean?"

"Serafina has to save herself," Joaquim said. "If she doesn't keep herself together, we won't be in time to help."

Alejandro managed to shove the blind aside before retching out the coach's window.

CHAPTER 5

Saturday, 26 June 1920

THE LAST REMNANTS of the fake spell circle could still be seen in the light of the setting sun, overlaid like a shimmering mirage atop the chevron-patterned paving stones of the square. Only a fine tracery now, earlier it would have been bright and alarming. The square lay in front of the magnificent baroque church of Bom Jesus; it was no small wonder that the priests had been offended when they found it. This was what had drawn Rafael away from the police station this morning, when Alejandro had wanted to talk to him.

Alejandro stood there with a terrible taste in his mouth. He wanted to pace, to work off some of his worry, but he felt queasy. Miguel didn't look much better. He leaned heavily on his cane, his narrow face pale. Neither of them was drunk any longer.

"Where do we go from here?" Alejandro asked Joaquim and Gaspar.

"I'm going to go sit on the bench," Joaquim answered. "I don't have a feel for her right now, but if I could concentrate, I might be able to pinpoint her the moment he lets his glamour loosen."

And that's our best hope? Alejandro surveyed the church. Phillips wouldn't have gone there, not if he was part fairy. They loathed holy ground. They hated moving water, which eliminated the banks of the Leça and the port. Everything around the Douro River as well. How much fairy blood did Phillips have?

Gaspar turned on Miguel. "If you read that version of the story, you're our best hope for remembering whether Jandro wrote all this down at some point. Think, man."

Suddenly put on the spot, Miguel frowned, eyes focusing inward. "I . . ."

A carriage pulled into the square at a quick clip. As it rolled to a stop, Rafael Pinheiro opened the door and jumped down without opening out the steps. Markovich followed at a slower pace, expression discontented. The swelling across his jaw had darkened to a livid blue in a few spots, a sign of how hard Roberto had hit him.

"Is that the Russian?" Miguel asked.

"He's English, but of Russian descent," Alejandro supplied.

"Hmmm." Miguel shook his head. "He has to be here."

Rafael approached the three of them standing near the spell circle, Markovich trailing him. "Miguel, what are you doing here?"

"Alejandro gave me a version of this story to edit, Father," Miguel said. "So I remember more than he does. I . . . I *know* more, so I'm here."

Rafael let out a colorful curse. "I should have asked myself about that. So what are we waiting for, Gaspar?"

"Joaquim is trying to get a feel for where Serafina is," Gaspar answered, then turned to Markovich. "What can you tell us about Phillips?"

"Not much," Markovich said.

"Not good enough," Gaspar responded. "You work for the English government, and he's an Irish separatist. They have to be gathering information on him. Given the threat he poses to you, I'm sure they kept you apprised."

"I don't know what I can tell you that you don't already know," Markovich said.

"The maledictor has to be here," Rafael said. "But I don't think he has any information. Son?"

He'd looked to Miguel as he said that.

Miguel closed his eyes, mumbling, "Story with a fairy . . . and a girl . . . and . . . I'm not sure what to say."

Alejandro wanted to shake Miguel for being so unhelpful. "What do you *mean* by that?"

Roberto returned to the square just then, a paper sack clutched in one hand. "Bread," he told Alejandro, holding out the bag. "You'll feel better if you get something into your stomach."

Ah, that was where Roberto went. The young man had been talking to Miguel, and then wandered off. Alejandro gave Roberto a heartfelt thanks and opened the bag. It held a loaf of sweet bread. His mouth began watering, and he reached to pull it out.

"Don't eat that," Miguel warned him. "We'll need that later."

"What is it, Miguel?"

"He's made a portal," Miguel said. "He'll threaten to throw his hostage through it. We need the bread for . . . for the fairy."

That *hostage* was Serafina. Why was Miguel being so coy about what he remembered? Alejandro folded the top of the bag closed. "What do we do then?"

"We have to find the portal," Miguel said. "He'll be there, waiting for us."

Gaspar stepped away from them and began sniffing the air.

"And how are we supposed to find it?" Alejandro asked.

"A fairy portal?" Markovich sneered. "Wait. You actually believe in these fairy stories?"

Halfway across the square to the church now, Gaspar stopped and said, "My wife is half fairy, son. We don't have to believe. We *know*."

Markovich surveyed the men gathered around him, mouth agape. "You're serious? All of you?"

"If you grow up knowing they exist," Miguel told him calmly, "there's nothing strange about it. Everyone believes sereia exist. Why should fairies be any different?"

Markovich gazed at Miguel with disbelief. "Who are you?"

"My son," Rafael inserted, giving Markovich a warning thump on his back.

Gaspar had returned to sniffing the air.

"Miguel, do you recall where the portal was supposed to be?" Joaquim asked then. "I'm not having any luck finding her."

"I don't, sir," Miguel said.

Alejandro scowled. Miguel had picked a terrible tidbit not to remember. He wanted to scream with frustration, but held it in. If he had his own gift, perhaps he would already be at Serafina's side. He couldn't blame Miguel.

Inspector Gaspar stood at one corner of the square now, head tilted back. Alejandro started toward him, hoping that Gaspar knew *something*. "Can you smell the portal, sir?"

"I'll need to get farther away from the remnants in the square," Gaspar said, "but I think this is the direction to go."

Alejandro went to join him, Joaquim and the others following, but Gaspar waved them back. "I need you to keep your distance. Especially you, Markovich. Your smells confuse the air."

Alejandro stopped where he was. Joaquim limped to stand next to him, the others spreading out about them.

"What is that man doing?" Markovich asked peevishly.

Joaquim sighed. "You are looking at the *meter*, son. You are seeing a magic so rare that God chose to give the world only one. He makes you look commonplace."

Apparently swayed by Joaquim's reverent tone, Markovich made his next comment softer. "He's a meter?"

"No," Joaquim said. "He's *the* meter. The only one."

"There have been meters before," Markovich objected.

"And they have all been *him*," Joaquim said softly.

Markovich gave Joaquim a disbelieving look. "You can't be serious. He's sniffing the air like a dog."

"Because he smells magic. I assume fairy magic has a different smell than human magic."

Gaspar had begun to walk along the sidewalk into the town—toward the Leça River. Alejandro followed, not interested in the academic discussion of Gaspar's abilities. Miguel limped at his side, unusually quiet, with Roberto on the other side. Alejandro noted that Miguel's limp was growing more marked. His lips were pressed in a thin line. "Will you make it there, Miguel?"

"If I have to crawl," Miguel snapped.

"You'll make it there," Roberto promised. "I'll see to it."

Gaspar turned down a side street, heading directly for what appeared to be a stable, and Alejandro *knew* that was the place. He ran across the cobbled courtyard, passing Gaspar and reaching the doors before any of the others.

"Careful!" Miguel yelled.

Alejandro flung the doors open, looking for Serafina. Instead, he saw a dozen carriage horses milling about inside. They wheeled about and ran straight at him to escape the stable.

Alejandro dove out of the way. He hit the wet cobbles of the stable's yard hard. Hooves clattered about him on the stone, terrifying in their closeness. His breath held; Alejandro tucked his arms about his head, making himself as small as possible. The beasts jumped over him, hooves hitting his back with thumps that jarred throughout his body.

"Jandro!" someone cried out.

For a moment, Alejandro just breathed. Other voices were calling out now, and the hooves sounded far away. He slowly uncurled, cringing when something in the vicinity of his ribs gave a sharp twinge of pain. *Stupid.*

He tried to push himself off the ground, but the pain in his ribs told him that wouldn't work.

Gaspar was at his side then, lifting him off the ground. "Broken?"

"I don't know," Alejandro gasped. It hurt; that was all he knew. He tried to pull away from Gaspar. "I have to get to her."

"Is he hurt?" Joaquim called.

"He'll live," Gaspar yelled back. "We wait, Jandro. We're stronger together."

Forced by the stabbing pain in his side, Alejandro waited while the others came to the stable doors. Gaspar picked up the bag that held the loaf of bread, or what was left of it. A hoof had landed squarely in the middle, savaging the paper and the loaf. "If we need this, we're pretty desperate."

"Is it in there?" Alejandro managed. "The portal?"

"Yes," Gaspar said. "I can feel it now. I don't know why this Phillips isn't making demands, though. He has the upper hand."

Alejandro didn't need to be reminded of that. Joaquim and Miguel had finally reached them. Markovich wore a worried look on his pale face. Roberto folded his arms over his chest, grim.

"Watch every word you say," Gaspar told them all. "Fairies are notoriously strict followers of their word, but they can also twist it around and use it against you."

"I remember," Joaquim said, mouth in a firm line.

"Unless this Phillips is a servant of the fairy who opened the portal, the fairy will treat him with the same fickleness it would use on us. Keep that in mind. They have their own loyalties and sometimes those loyalties don't make sense to humans. So be cautious."

Alejandro nodded. "Let's go."

Gaspar led the way. No matter how much Alejandro wanted to be in there first, he grasped the logic of letting Gaspar go ahead. If Phillips unleashed something, it wouldn't affect Gaspar. Alejandro limped along behind him, suddenly aware that his left leg had been hit by a hoof as well. Likely just a bruise, but it hurt fiercely. Roberto came and wrapped an arm around Alejandro's shoulders, steadying him as they walked into the stable.

Alejandro's skin crawled. At the far end of the stable in the middle of the aisle, he could see what had frightened the horses. A large hole glowed in the air, showing sunlight amidst of ring of strangely shifting flame. On the other side, a wheat field trembled in a summer breeze. Alejandro could feel, even twenty feet away, that it was *unnatural.* His teeth ached just looking at it. That was why the horses had scattered.

Serafina stood before it, facing a man Alejandro didn't recognize.

He could only see the man in profile, but nothing about him seemed special, nothing striking. The man was of average height and unremarkable coloring. His clothes looked like a countryman's garb. He held one hand outstretched. If he stepped one foot closer, it would be locked about Serafina's throat. Alejandro swallowed, his breath held.

She was singing. Very softly, so quietly that he couldn't hear the words. But they weren't meant for him anyway. She was using her *call* to hold Phillips in check.

How many hours has she held him there?

Alejandro swallowed again. For a sereia to use her powers continuously was exhausting. It required mental focus, and the sereia had to mine her own feelings to evoke a response in her target. Phillips, with his purported fairy blood, might be even more difficult to enspell than a human, yet he didn't even seem aware that they'd entered the stable.

This was what Joaquim meant when he'd said Serafina had to save herself.

She continued to sing, her lips moving and her gills flaring. If Phillips got a hand around her neck, he could stop her *call* by crushing her gills. She would never fully recover from that. Her voice would be ruined.

Alejandro's stomach felt like lead. "Don't distract her," he whispered.

No one moved.

"That isn't a fairy," Gaspar said softly. "He's not a witch of any kind."

"What do you mean, Uncle?"

Gaspar took a deep breath, his eyes narrowed. "There's a small vial on a chain around his neck. Do you see it? That's a fairy trap. He's using that to create the portal. We break the vial, the fairy will escape and the portal will close. If the fairy *wants* to escape. May not want to. It may be there voluntarily. Rafael?"

Rafael closed his eyes. "The vial will be broken," he said, "but the fairy can't aid us."

"Why not?" Roberto hissed.

"She will be too weak," Miguel answered, eyes turning to meet Roberto's. "In the story, that's why you bought the bread, Roberto. To feed the fairy so she'll survive."

Roberto mouth set in a grim line. "I understand."

Miguel's shoulders slumped a bit, as if that pronouncement had defeated him somehow. "Alejandro, it has to be him, not you. Fairies respond best to offerings from humans."

And I'm not entirely human. Alejandro gazed down at the trampled bag in his hand and handed it over to Roberto. "We have to do something. Soon."

"We plan," Gaspar said. "Serafina's buying us time, so let's use that time wisely."

By the time Gaspar had a plan, Alejandro was ready to scream with frustration. It seemed like hours had passed. Every time he glanced that direction, Phillips' hand was closer to Serafina's neck. And he was next to useless in Gaspar's plan. He wanted to break Phillips' hands or punch the man's face. Instead he was supposed to wait to one side while Gaspar and Markovich did all the work. Even Roberto had more of a part in the plan than he did.

Gaspar walked toward the open portal. Alejandro followed, Roberto on one side, Rafael beyond him. Joaquim and Miguel were left behind to guard the stable doors, in case something went wrong . . . or in case one of Phillips' henchmen should turn up. Markovich was there as the last line of defense.

Phillips' hand was only an inch from Serafina's throat.

As they got closer, Serafina's song made it hard to move. Hard to do anything. But Gaspar—immune to her *call*—walked right up to the frozen duo and shoved Phillips away from Serafina.

Serafina's song stopped, and she stumbled backward. Alejandro managed to get his arms around her before she fainted, even though taking her weight made his ribs scream in pain. He broke out in a cold sweat.

Gaspar's weight carried Phillips to the straw-coated floor of the stable. Roberto jumped on the man as well, using his knife to saw at the leather strip around the man's neck. Panicked, Phillips grabbed at him, but Roberto cut the vial free, rolled away, and rose.

Rafael planted his foot atop Phillips' chest and then leaned over him. "Don't move."

Alejandro ended up sitting on the floor, cradling Serafina and wishing fervently that they were farther from the portal. His skin crawled with the wrongness of it. And it continued to blaze unnatural light into the stable, as if it was noon on the other side.

"Don't be a fool!" Phillips protested.

Rafael leaned, putting more of his weight on the Irishman's chest. "Don't talk, either."

Roberto peered at the vial in his hand, some decision warring in his mind.

Miguel had abandoned his spot by the doors, and now stood near Roberto. "Open it, Roberto."

Roberto carefully pried out the metal stopper and reverently laid the vial on the stable floor. A pale light flowed over the ground, moving toward where Alejandro and Serafina sat.

Alejandro began dragging Serafina away. She woke and struggled for a second, and then she was halfway dragging *him*. "What is that?" she asked in a rasping voice.

Once they were a dozen feet away, Alejandro turned back to see Roberto tearing off bits of bread, saying something over them—a blessing, he thought—and dropping them into the cloud where they faded from sight.

Slowly, the cloud spread, becoming larger and more opaque until it took the form of a young woman in tattered garb, bedraggled and scarred. She covered her face with thin fingers and keened softly.

Alejandro had always thought fairies were supposed to be beautiful. What had scarred her? And why did this strike some chord of memory in him? Had he read a story—written a story—like this before?

"Can she close that portal?" Gaspar asked, a note of concern in his usually calm voice. "Before it eats us?"

Alejandro realized that the portal had grown larger, as if freeing her from that vial had removed all constraints on it. What would happen if it continued to grow?

Roberto knelt down, trying to see her face. He ignored the portal. "I don't think she can."

"Machado, that girl isn't human," Gaspar said, not taking his eyes from Phillips. "Be careful."

Roberto touched the girl's hands, gently pulled them away from her face. Her skin was crossed over and over with scars. "Can you help us?" Roberto asked. "We need to close the portal, but none of us can do that. Only you can."

She shuddered, and reality shuddered with her. "I don't have the strength," she whispered. "Not after so long in that iron prison."

Now that Alejandro looked, he could see that the glass vial encased a tracery of metal wires. Fairies hated iron, so that must have been torture.

"What would it take, lady?" Roberto asked her, the flickering edge of the portal almost lapping at his heels now.

"A sacrifice," she whispered, eyes lifting to meet his.

"Then take me."

"Machado, no!" Gaspar jumped toward Roberto, but not fast enough to forestall his offer.

Serafina grabbed at Alejandro's hand, her face alarmed. "What. . . ?"

The portal closed, dropping the stable into darkness. There were no lanterns still lit, and the twilight was too deep now to provide much light. But Roberto and the girl were gone.

"What just happened?" Alejandro asked in the sudden silence.

"That pork-and-beans stole my frigging fairy," Phillips snarled. He grabbed at Rafael's foot and shoved hard. Off balance, Rafael fell to the floor with an *oof*. Phillips rolled to his feet, shoved Miguel out of his way, and ran, heading for the stable door and the twilight outside.

Markovich blocked the doorway. "I don't think so, Irish."

Phillips stopped halfway, breathing hard. "Where are my diamonds, you damned Tan?"

Alejandro disentangled himself from Serafina's arms and rose stiffly to his feet. "He doesn't have them."

In the dim light of the stable, Phillips turned to Alejandro. "And you do?"

"No." Alejandro set one hand to his aching ribs. "I gave them to a girl in Armentières."

Phillips' hands balled into fists. He stepped closer. "You did what?"

"I gave them to a girl," Alejandro repeated. "In Armentières."

Phillips' lip curled in a sneer. "You never intended to split them with us, did you?"

"No," Alejandro said. "I never did. I'm not a thief."

Phillips took a step toward Alejandro. "But you were willing to give them to some whore?"

"Whore?" Alejandro repeated with a short laugh. "No. I gave them to the mail girl. She posted them to the Holy Sisters in Poperinge, for the orphanage that was bombed there."

"You what?" Phillips lunged toward Alejandro.

While Alejandro was talking, Markovich had come up behind Phillips and now grasped the back of the man's jacket in one first. He held out the other hand as if to strike Phillips.

This was *not* the plan.

"Stop!" Rafael yelled. "We need to arrest him, English. Not turn him inside out."

Phillips eyes went hostile, teeth exposed in a snarl. He tried to tug away from Markovich. "You won't get me inside an English prison."

"No we won't." Miguel still sat on his rump where Phillips had knocked him down. "But you *will* face justice. The punishment you deserve."

Alejandro shot a confused glance at Miguel.

"Wait," Miguel said, gesturing for him to remain still.

Blinding light spread across the stable, the portal opening once more. Phillips stumbled backward into Markovich, who roughly shoved him toward the portal.

In a blaze of white, a man waited on the other side. The man had a streak of gray in his dark hair, starting where a scar crossed his face. Alejandro gasped.

Time must pass differently in the fairy realm. He was looking at Roberto Machado . . . only years older. It still seemed to be full day there, but Roberto stood in a forest now, pines and larches growing tall behind him. And at a distance, a woman waited. Wind tugged at her gown and hair, but she still covered her face with her hands.

"She wants him," Roberto said, lifting his chin. "Bring him to me."

Alejandro wasn't sure to whom Roberto was speaking, but Markovich took advantage of everyone's shock to shove Phillips that direction again. Phillips turned and hissed at him, raising one hand.

"Without your fairy, you're nothing more than a petty thief," Markovich said. "I'm not scared of you."

Phillips lunged at the Englishman, mouth twisted in fear. Markovich stepped neatly out of the man's way, one hand touching Phillip's back as he passed. Phillips stopped midlunge, as if held in place by unseen ropes. "What have you done?" he screamed.

Markovich stepped back. "I cursed you. Whatever did you expect, you toe rag?"

Phillips' dark eyes were wide as he hung there. "What?"

"You will face the thing you fear the most," Markovich said in a nasty voice. "Apparently fairies are real, and now I know that's true, I have to wonder if they're as vengeful as people say. Always some truth in myth, I've heard."

The unseen ropes tugged on Phillips' frozen form, drawing him closer to the portal. "No!"

Markovich stepped up and pushed the Irishman hard. Phillips spun back toward the portal, control lost. He spun as if caught in a whirlwind, and grew smaller and smaller until he flew through the portal. On the other side, Roberto held up one hand, a vial in it, and as they watched, Phillips was sucked inside, silenced.

Roberto tucked the cap into the vial, and then secreted the thing inside his jacket. "It was not just him," he said. "Generations of his family held her captive, going back hundreds of years. She has first claim on him for his crimes."

Gaspar and Rafael looked inclined to argue that. But neither did.

Miguel struggled to rise and made his way to the portal. "Roberto, was it the right choice?"

Roberto laughed softly and raised one hand. "I have never regretted it, Miguel. I am happy to serve my lady. I am her champion and trusted friend. Thank you for warning me. I would not have thought to offer otherwise."

Alejandro's mind reeled. Hadn't he read that somewhere? Something about a fairy lady and her scarred champion. Hadn't there been stories. . . ?

"No, I think you would have anyway, Roberto. It's in your nature," Miguel said. "God be with you."

Roberto smiled and, with one swipe of his hand, caused the portal to close. The stable dropped back into darkness, the smell of burned straw and pine needles the only evidence that anything had happened.

"What just happened?" Markovich flicked open a lighter, sending a ghastly glow across his features.

"Roberto rescued a fairy," Miguel said, "and ran off to live another life. An adventure where he gets to be valiant and win a war for her." He turned to Alejandro.

"We wrote stories about that, when we were boys just learning to read, of the fairy lady who wouldn't show her face. They were improbable things, but they were *our* stories, Jandro. Yet perhaps . . . they were Roberto's all along."

He could remember the stories now. Not writing them, but Alejandro could remember the tales themselves, clearly products of young boys' imaginations. Or perhaps not. "I remember them."

"I got to be you today," Miguel said. "I was the one who knew what would happen. I was the seer." He took a deep breath. "I set Roberto on that path, and only for a few minutes was I uncertain of his fate, the story I *made* him believe in. But those few minutes were terrifying. I never want that sort of responsibility again."

Alejandro coughed and then wrapped his arms about his sides, wheezing. "And I never want to be run over by horses again. I'll leave that to you."

Gaspar groaned. "I suppose we have some horses to find. Joaquim, can you help me with that." Together they left the stables, Rafael going with them, to corral the runaway horses.

Markovich sat down on the floor of the stable, hands between his knees. "It's over," he said in English. "Thank God."

Yes, this meant Markovich no longer need look over his shoulder for assassins. Alejandro was glad it had turned out well for the Englishman. He turned about, looking for his own reward. Serafina raised her hands and he helped her up, ignoring the twinge in his ribs as he did so. He set his hands on her elbows and met her eyes. "Did he hurt you?"

She gazed up at him. "No. I'm . . . I'm not hurt. Just . . . I feel exhausted."

He stroked a curl back from her forehead, and tugged out a stray piece of hay. "I am sorry he ever touched you. If I had known, I would have just given him his damned diamonds that day long ago."

She smiled weakly and leaned into him, and Alejandro just clenched his jaw and wrapped his arms around her. The twinging ribs, the burning in his calf . . . none of that mattered. He had her back safe and he was never going to let her go again.

Friday, 1 July 1921

All three of their names appeared on the book. During the year since Roberto's disappearance, Alejandro and Miguel had worked together to rewrite many of their old stories, and Serafina had contributed several poems to the volume. She'd insisted that in some of the stories, the fairy lady must rescue her champion rather than the other way around, a challenge Alejandro and Miguel had been happy to accept.

Several of the stories had been serialized in the Porto Gazette over the previous three months, building an appetite for the collection. *The Fairy Lady* sold well on its first day, crowds coming into the Lello Bookstore to pick up their copies and find out what happened to the fairy who wouldn't show her face and her scarred human champion.

That evening, after the store closed its doors to customers, Miguel and Alejandro stood on the middle level of the stairwell, overlooking the great store, Serafina at Alejandro's side. Their publisher—a friend of the Duke of Coimbra, of course—raised his glass of champagne and saluted their debut. "To the writers of my newest success, may we see many more volumes of the fairy lady's adventures."

"To Roberto Machado!" Alejandro responded.

"Roberto," Serafina and Miguel agreed. They had all agreed that the book would be dedicated to him. Their families could wait until the next volume.

Later that evening, after their publisher had taken them to a congratulatory dinner and Miguel had returned to visit his parents' house to tell them of their success—and to see Isabella, no doubt—Alejandro sat on the balcony outside the bedroom window at the house on the Street of Flowers. A light rain fell, not much more than a mist, and he listened to the traffic heading up and down the street, his eyes half closed. The electric tram rattled by, automobiles and carriages and oxen contributing their sounds to the underlying drone. Alejandro found the sounds calming.

Everything had worked out, fortunately. A telegram from the Sint Janskerk in Poperinge verified that an anonymous donor had sent them a large quantity of diamonds in 1918, marked for their orphans, so the diamonds had gone where Alejandro intended. No longer looking over his shoulder, Markovich had returned to work for his government. Miguel was now editing for the Gazette, and had forgiven Alejandro the thing he'd said years before.

And Serafina knew that she had a husband who loved her, no matter how rocky the beginning of their marriage had been. That was the thing Alejandro had wished for most.

She's coming.

A moment later, Serafina stepped out onto the balcony next to him. She leaned down to press a kiss to his hair and wrap her arms around his neck. "Shall we go in to bed?"

He'd known she would say that. Not because she often did, but because he *knew*.

He could hear it now, his seer's gift. It whispered to him, only hints of the future. He was content to let it stay that way. He had used it to serve long enough. For now, like a soldier retired from the wars, he would enjoy the present and all the joys it brought.

THE END

Cast of Characters

Alejandro (Alexandre) Ferreira, Jandro—son of Alexandre Ferreira and Leandra Rocha, half sereia, half human, seer.

Ana (Santos), Duchess of Coimbra

Bastião—former guard for the current Duke of Coimbra

Duilio Ferreira—eldest living brother of Alejandro Ferreira

Isabella Anjos—daughter of Gabriel Anjos and Nadezhda Vladimirova, healer

James Markovich—Englishman of Russian ancestry, maledictor

Jandro—nickname for Alejandro (J is pronounced like an H)

João—character in story written by a young Alejandro Ferreira

João da Silva—name used for an unknown man in Portugal

Joaquim Tavares, Inspector—Alejandro's elder brother, finder

the Lady—half-fairy, wife of Miguel Gaspar

Lighter—English witch, assigned to work with Alejandro during the war, firestarter

Marcos Davila—half sereia of Spanish birth, Serafina's
    father

Mariona Palmeira—younger sister of Serafina

Marina Arenias—sereia, Alejandro's adoptive mother

Mendosa (Luis)—Ferreira family butler

Miguel Gaspar, Inspector—mestiço from Cabo Verde,
    husband of the Lady

Miguel Pinheiro—adopted son of Captain Rafael Pinheiro

Phillips—Irish Separatist, assigned to work with
    Alejandro during the war

Rafael Pinheiro, Captain—cousin of Alejandro, seer

Raimundo, Duke of Coimbra

Roberto Machado—footman in the Ferreira house, war
    veteran

Safira Palmeira—Serafina's mother

Serafina (Serafim) Palmeira—eldest daughter of Safira
    Palmeira and Marcos Davila, sereia

A few Portuguese words

Baixa—downtown (specifically, downtown Lisboa)

fado—traditional Portuguese music form, characterized
    by mournful tunes and lyrics

mestiço—individual of mixed blood (in this instance,
    Portuguese/African)

praça—plaza

Vinho Verde—young Portuguese wine (literally 'green
    wine')

ALEJANDRO'S CHARTS

Ferreira Family Chart
(Filho = Son, Neto = Grandson)

Alexandre Ferreira ———— Alessio Ferreira ———— Segu (selkie)
   m. Giana Fadda   with Tigana

                                Duilio Ferreira   ———— Lygia
                                  m. Oriana Paredes ———— Giana
                                                      Isabel

with Rosa Quintana ————Joaquim Tavares Filho ———— Rosa
(Tavares)   m. Marina Arenias ———— Felipa
                                                   Alma
                                                       Felis
                                                      Joaquim Neto

with Leandra Rocha ———— Alejandro Ferreira
                              m. Serafina Palmeira

Other Children:
Giana Fadda   ———— Erdano
   with Guidano (selkie)   multiple children with multiple mates

Rosa Quintana   ———— Cristiano Tavares ———— Luciano
   m. Joaquim Tavares   m. Emília (Emily) Atkinson

Leandra Rocha   ———— Liliana Rocha (my half-sister!)
   with William Adler

(Half-brother of Alexandre)
  Paolo Silva   ———— Rafael Pinheiro   ———— Miguel
     with Antonia Pinheiro   m. Genoveva Jardim ———— Emilio
                                               Tiago

Author's Note

THE BATTLE OF LA LYS (WW1) was terrible for the Portuguese. The German army sent several Divisions with tanks up against one exhausted division of Portuguese (who had been on the front line for eight months and were scheduled to be moved to the rear the next day.) The Portuguese Second Division was, therefore, only at partial strength when the Germans attacked. It had been 20,000 men, but attrition had reduced that number to as low as 15,000. Accounts vary, but in their 2001 book, Mendo Castro Henriques and Antonio Rosas Leitão gave the numbers as: dead (1,341), wounded (4,626), missing (1,932), and prisoners (7,440).

Much of the information I gathered about this particular battle came from the master's thesis of Jesse Pyles, THE PORTUGUESE EXPEDITIONARY CORPS IN WORLD WAR I: FROM INCEPTION TO COMBAT DESTRUCTION, 1914–1918. Mr. Pyles did a ton of research from which I profited, and I greatly appreciate the work that went into his paper. Thank you, sir.

The Lello Bookstore in Porto is regularly listed among the most beautiful bookstores in the world. It now charges an admission fee (too many tourists!) but the price is minimal.

Finally, a note about a voluntary historical inaccuracy: the *Café Elite* didn't open until December of 1921, but I hoped it wouldn't be too much of a stretch of credulity to have it open the previous year. It changed its name in 1922 to the *Café Majestic*, under which it still operates today. If you're ever in Porto, its Art-Nouveau beauty makes it well worth a visit.

About the Author

J. KATHLEEN CHENEY is A former teacher and has taught mathematics ranging from 7th grade to Calculus, with a brief stint as a Gifted and Talented Specialist. She is a member of SFWA, RWA, and Broad Universe. Her works have been published in *Jim Baen's Universe*, *Writers of the Future XXIV*, *Beneath Ceaseless Skies,* and *Fantasy Magazine,* among others.

To find excerpts of her work, short fiction, and to sign up for her mailing list, visit *www.jkathleencheney.com.*

An EQP Book

E-QUALITY PRESS
http://EQPBooks.com/

Made in the USA
Monee, IL
26 May 2020